Tucker

**Center Point
Large Print**

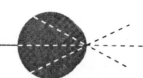

**This Large Print Book carries the
Seal of Approval of N.A.V.H.**

Tucker

Louis L'Amour

Center Point Publishing
Thorndike, Maine

This Center Point Large Print edition
is published in the year 2006 by arrangement with
Bantam Books, an imprint of The Bantam Dell Publishing Group,
a division of Random House, Inc.

The text of this Large Print edition is unabridged. In other
aspects, this book may vary from the original edition.
Printed in the United States of America.
Set in 16-point Times New Roman type.

ISBN 1-58547-699-4

Library of Congress Cataloging-in-Publication Data

L'Amour, Louis, 1908-
   Tucker / Louis L'Amour.--Center Point large print ed.
      p. cm.
   ISBN 1-58547-699-4 (lib. bdg. : alk. paper)
   1. Large type books. I. Title.

PS3523.A446T83 2005
813'.52--dc22
                                                                      2005019956

To
REX MARTINDALE,
of
Montana,
Wyoming,
and
California

Tucker

CHAPTER 1

When I rode up to the buffalo wallow pa was lying there with his leg broke and his horse gone.

It was mid-afternoon of a mighty hot day and pa had been lying there three, four hours. His canteen was on his horse, so he had nothing to drink in all that time. I got down and fetched him water with my canteen.

"Thanks, boy. Looks like I played hob."

"Well," I said, "you got you a busted leg, but your jaw's in good shape. You been arguin' at me for months, now, so you just set back an' argue some more whilst I fix up your leg."

"You got to saddle and ride, boy." A body could see he was fighting pain. "Everything we own and most of what our neighbors own is in those saddlebags. You just forget about me and hunt down that horse."

If I'd been older in years instead of being just man-size I might have thought about the money first, but likely not. There was twenty thousand dollars in those saddlebags, and less than a third of it was ours. It was the sale money for a steer herd we'd driven up the trail from Texas, and folks back home was a-sweating until we got back with that money.

"We'll take care of your busted leg first," I said.

There was mighty little to do with out there on the prairie, but I broke some mesquite and trimmed it with my knife, shaping some splints for pa's leg.

9

We'd never been much on gettin' along together, pa an' me, and we wrangled most of the time on something or other. Here I was, seventeen and feeling uppity with the growing strength in me and the need to make folks see me as a man. About all I could do, come to think about it, was ride a horse and shoot a gun.

Pa objected to the company I kept, and down deep inside I more'n half agreed with him, but stubborn-like, I wasn't going to be told. Pa objected to me spending time out in the gully practicing gun-slinging. He was forever telling me that no gunman he'd ever heard tell of ever had anything but a bad reputation with folks who mattered.

"Time of trouble," I objected, "a man who can handle a gun is good to have around, and on your side."

"Sure," pa would say, "but when trouble is over folks can't get shut of him fast enough."

Well, I'd always told myself I could make as big tracks as any man, but now I was faced up with it and had no idea what to do.

One thing I knew. I needed a water hole and some shade for pa. Once he was bedded down I could high-tail it after that horse. The quickest way to water might be to trail pa's horse, anyway, so I hoisted him into the saddle with some help from him, and we'd taken after pa's gelding.

That fool horse ran straightaway, then slowed to a walk. From time to time we could see where the horse stopped to look back, or to nibble on some mesquite or such. When the tracks began to edge off toward the southwest I was hopeful he was headed for water.

Pa sat up in the saddle and he didn't say aye, yes, or no. This was up to me now, and we both knew it, and he held his jaw. It had me feeling guilty and responsible all at the same time. And then an hour short of sundown we fetched up to some other tracks.

They came in from the northwest and they were shod horses. Three in the bunch . . . and they'd caught pa's horse.

Half the outlaws in the country lived in that part of the territory, and the chances were that anybody riding across here was an outlaw, or kin to them. Not to say that many a man who passes for honest wouldn't help himself to twenty thousand dollars and a lost horse.

"Don't you take notions, son. You ain't about to go up against three men. Not with me in this condition."

It was shy of sundown when we came to the creek. It wasn't much. Two, three feet wide and a few inches deep, running through a sparse meadow between low-growing willows, with here and there a clump of cottonwood. When I had pa off his horse and bedded down, I unslung my canteen and filled it at the creek.

"You set quiet, pa. I'll go fetch that horse."

"Don't be a fool, Edwin. You stay here."

Pa never called me Edwin unless he was mad or upset, and it was plain to be seen now that he was a worried man. Well, I was some worried my ownself.

Pa had always taken on about what it meant to have

a good name, and how a man was judged by the company he kept. Whenever he saw me strutting it around with Doc Sites, Kid Reese, and them, he would read the riot act to me.

They bragged they had rustled cows, and maybe they had. They never worked that I could see, but they always had them a few dollars, which was more than I could say, and pa kept me working morning until night.

For the first time I was beginning to understand what it might mean to have a good name. If we showed up back home without that money some folks would believe our story, but others would recall that I'd been trailing around with Doc Sites and Kid Reese, and they would talk it up. Some others would come to believe there'd been something wrong, and the first thing you knew they'd give pa a bad name as well as me.

We'd never had much. When I was born pa lived back east, but after a bad time he came west and got himself some land of his own. Fire burned him out that fall, and the following spring he put in a crop with borrowed seed, and the grasshoppers taken the crop.

He worked almighty hard, but two years of drought followed, and we lost the place. I've heard folks talk as if anybody who didn't have money must be no-account, but they didn't know some of the hard-working folks I'd known.

We moved to Texas then and filed on a claim and worked like dogs for three years. We built a house and a barn, and got a couple hundred head of stock. Then Comanches raided us, burned us out, and ran off the stock. They killed my Uncle Bud that time.

The herd we had just sold was the first we'd been able to put together, and once we got home with that money we'd have an edge on the future for the first time. We were headed home when pa and me had a big argument and I rode off and left him, mad as all get-out and swearing not to come back.

Only a few hours later I did turn back, and lucky I did. Pa's horse had shied at a rattler and throwed him, breaking his leg. If I hadn't quit sulking and turned back he might have died right there.

Had I been with him I could have caught up his horse and we'd have only the broke leg to worry about. As it was we stood to lose all we had, and all our friends had as well, and they'd trusted us.

Well, anyway, I taken after our horse and those men, and hadn't gone more than a mile from where I'd left pa before I smelled smoke. They had them a fire under some cottonwoods alongside that same creek where I'd left pa, and before they saw me coming I'd recognized them. It was Doc Sites, Kid Reese, and a square-shouldered man in a cowhide vest and a black hat. That had to be Bob Heseltine.

How many stories had Doc and the Kid told me about him? He was, they said, the best rider, the best shot, and the fastest man with a gun anywhere around. Bob Heseltine had held up the Garston Bank. He had killed Sheriff Baker in a gun battle. He had, they said, made two Texas Rangers back down. All they talked about was Bob Heseltine and the big things they'd do when he got back . . . and here he was.

He was a mite shorter than me but wide in the shoulders, and the hide of his face was like tanned leather. He wore his gun tied down, and a body could see he was a mighty tough man.

There was pa's horse, still saddled. The saddlebags were off and the money dumped on the blanket. They would be some disappointed when they saw me riding up to claim it.

"Howdy!" I called out, riding into camp.

Fixed on the money as they were, they jumped for their guns, ready to fight.

Kid Reese relaxed when he saw me. "It's all right, Bob. He's a friend of ours."

"I see you found pa's horse." I was mighty dry in the mouth, all of a sudden. "And our money."

Heseltine turned his head around at me, real slow. His hard blue eyes looked mean at you over high cheekbones. Doc's lips kind of thinned down, and Kid Reese taken a slow breath, just a-staring at me. Firelight flickered on their faces, on the shining flanks of their horses, and on the gold and silver coins heaped on the blanket. It flickered off their gun barrels, too.

"What d'you mean? *Your* money?" Heseltine demanded. "This here is our money."

"Hey, now!" I objected. "Look—"

"You look." Heseltine fixed me with those hard blue

14

eyes. "I never seen you before. You come ridin' in here and lay claim to our money. You ain't about to get it. Not a lousy two-bits worth."

"They know me." I indicated Doc and the Kid. "And they know that horse. Pa bought that horse in East Texas, and has papers on him. The Kid knows that horse—he's seen me ride him often enough. And that's pa's saddle."

Nobody said anything, and suddenly I was scared. Sure, me and the Kid and Doc, we had talked big of robberies and such, but that was fool kid talk . . . or was it?

"That's his pa's horse, all right," Reese admitted. "You shut your trap," Heseltine said.

"That money belongs to us and to the folks back home," I said. "You know that, Doc."

"Hell," Doc said, "they never did nothing for me back there."

"You could come in with us," Reese suggested. "Just like we planned it would be when Bob came back. We can start right from here, the four of us—but with money."

We had done some talking about rustling cattle and robbing stages or banks, but now they wanted to steal our money, the money pa and me and our neighbors had sweated for. Right then I began to take a different view of things. It was one thing to talk of being bandits, but I guess I'd never really thought of it as anything but talk. Now I could see how it hurt a man to be robbed of what he'd worked hard for.

"Pa's back up the creek with his leg broke," I said, not thinking how much I was giving away to them. "I've got to get back to him with that horse and the money."

Bob Heseltine was facing me. "You may have been a friend to the boys here, but you're not taking any money away from here. Not you nor anybody else."

All three of them were facing me, all squared away to make their fight. Kid Reese was suddenly grinning like a fool. He'd always looked down on me, anyway. Doc had a rifle in his hands, and Heseltine had laid it on the line for them.

They stood ready to kill me. And these were the boys I'd been hanging out with all summer. These were the friends I'd defended to my pa.

They had me euchred. Pa, he used to tell me that when a man was holding the wrong cards it was always better not to try to buck the game. It was better to throw in your cards and wait for another deal.

Only thing I was wondering now was, would they let me get out of here?

"You won't be needin' pa's horse," I said.

I caught up the reins and rode out of there, but it was all seeming unreal to me. I was expecting any minute to get a bullet in the back. It was Heseltine who worried me. Then I heard Reese say, "You ain't goin' to let him ride off? He'll have the law on us."

"For what? For finding money?" But I kept on going.

Riding back to where pa lay, I kept telling myself

that if it hadn't been for pa I'd have shot it out with them, but way down deep I wasn't so sure.

Pa was setting up, his back against a tree. He looked mighty relieved when I rode in, but his face was gray and drawn. He was surely in pain. So I built us a fire and made coffee whilst I told him about it.

"Son, we've got to get our money. Folks trusted us with their stock, an' we given our word."

So I explained about Bob Heseltine, who was maybe as tough as Wild Bill Hickok.

"Who says so, boy? Those two-by-twice hitch-rack outlaws? Neither Sites nor Reese would know a tough man if they saw one."

"I saw him. He sizes up mighty mean."

Pa looked at me out of those level gray eyes of his. Old eyes, I suddenly realized. I'd never thought of pa as old, but he was. I'd been a son born to his later years.

"How tough are you, boy?" he asked now.

"Me?" I was startled. I'd never thought of myself as really tough. Well, I take that back. Time to time down in the gully where I'd practiced with a six-shooter I had told myself what I'd do if faced with trouble . . . only this here was no daydream. "Why, I don't know. I guess a man has to find out."

What surprised me more than anything was pa suggesting I might be tough. He'd always played that down.

"You're right, son. You never know how tough a man is until you've tried him. Edwin, you he'p me up on that horse. We're a-goin' back."

"You got you a broke leg."

"My trigger finger ain't broke." Pa, he looked at me. "Edwin, you and me worked side by side doing the work of five or six men to put that herd together. We taken it up the trail short-handed. We held it together against Indians, hailstorms, and stampede. We taken it over land and through water and we ate dust and went through hell to do it.

"Now those three are takin' it from us, three men who were never good for anything, nor did an honest day's work in their lives. If a man won't fight for what is rightly his, if he won't fight for what he believes, then he ain't much account. We're goin' back up there, you and me, and if it's fight they want they've bought themselves a packet."

Well, I just looked at him. I'd never seen pa like that, nor believed he had it in him. I'd seen him fight Indians from inside a house, but I'd never seen him r'ar up all teeth an' talon like this.

All of a sudden I was wondering how I'd measure up when the showdown came . . . and to think I'd been low-rating pa all this time.

They were gone. There was a thin smoke from a dying fire, and some trampled sod, but they had taken out.

"Scared," pa said, contempt in his tone, "scared of a boy and a man with a broke leg. We got to catch them."

"Look, pa, you're in no shape to ride. We can go home and—"

"Boy, what're you talkin' about? It's a week's ride to the ranch, three days to the nearest folks we know. If they get that much start we'll never catch them."

They did not sleep that night, I was sure, and neither did we. The moon was high and white, the cap-rock prairies like a floor covered with thin grass. The tracks were there, the only marks across that grass where nothing had walked since the buffalo passed.

Pa sat straight in his saddle. He neither whimpered nor groaned. When we watered in a coulee with day a-coming I thought I'd never seen a man so drawn and tight, yet all the night long he had followed a trail that was scarcely more than a shadow on the grass.

There in that coulee I helped pa down and covered him with a blanket. He slept some, so I unsaddled the horses and let them roll in the dust, then picketed them out. I lay down, just to relax a mite, and when I opened my eyes the sun was over the horizon in the east.

Pa floundered into a sitting position and I scouted buffalo chips to make a fire. Careful to make no smoke, for this was Comanche country, I made coffee and sliced bacon into a skillet.

"We got to find a place," I said. "You surely need rest."

"I spent more years in the saddle than on my back, son, and if I die it'll be in the saddle."

When I helped him into the saddle again I accidentally bumped his leg and he winced, his face went white, and sweat started from his forehead. Ashamed of my clumsiness, I climbed aboard the hammer-headed roan I was riding.

That horse was not one a man would choose a-purpose. He was raw-boned and no-account-looking and he had a devil in his eye, but he could go all night and the next morning, then give him a few mouthfuls of antelope bush or bunchgrass and a hatful of water, and he'd be off and going again.

All the time I kept thinking what would happen when we fetched up to Heseltine and them. There was nothing behind me that made me fit to buck the likes of them. I said as much.

"You can be as tough as you're of a mind to be, son. I've watched you, boy. I've watched you work and seen you ride the rough string, and you've got all any man has got. I've seen you handle that gun, too, and you're good, boy, mighty good. I know nothing about Heseltine, but there's nothing in Sites or Reese that need worry you."

Pa had never said a word of praise to me that I could recall. Nor had I any idea he'd seen me practicing with a gun. But he had to be wrong. I'd never fought with any man, with either knuckle or gun.

Heseltine was a hard man. I won't deny the clothes he wore added to it. There was a swagger about him. My clothes were nothing. I'd never owned a store-bought suit. I had a shirt my shoulders were begin-ning to split, and I'd outgrown my jeans two summers

20

ago. My boots were down-at-heel.

The wind was raw and cold on the high plains. Hunching our shoulders, we pushed against it, riding a land that offered us nothing but prairie and sky.

We had only their tracks to guide us, and the anger that grew more terrible as the hours drew on. Pa sat up in his saddle and made no sound. His cheeks hollowed down and his eyes sank back into his skull, but the light in them scared me. If I was Bob Heseltine I'd be a worried man.

"You've got the makin's, Edwin," he said suddenly. "You'll make big tracks on the land. There was a Texas Ranger once who said there was no stoppin' a man who knew he was in the right and kept a-comin'."

Big tracks on the land. They were words he used of few men, only such as Jim Bowie, Sam Houston, Goodnight, and Slaughter.

Pa began to speak of them, telling me stories of the Goodnight-Loving Trail, of mountain men, trail drivers, and Texas Rangers. Of ancestors of ours who fought with the Green Mountain Boys, of Decatur and Andy Jackson, and all sorts of people and things I'd never guessed he knew of. Alongside of some of those men, Bob Heseltine didn't sound like much; all the stories I'd heard of him began to sound like a man hollering into an empty rain barrel—the sound coming back, but nothing there.

Cold, spitting rain began to fall, the tracks grew faint. From time to time we'd find a hoof-print, the stub of a cigarette, or some small thing to mark their passing.

Pa's leg looked awful. It was swollen around the splint, but he wouldn't let me touch it. He'd taken his knife and slit his pants-leg to ease the pressure, and toward nightfall he asked me to split his boot. His gasp of relief when I done it told me how awful the pain had been before.

When I got back into the saddle it came over me all of a sudden that pa wasn't going to make it.

I knew then that he knew it, too. He was just hanging on, hoping we'd come up with them whilst he could stand beside me at the showdown. He would get back the money he'd been trusted with, and he could leave me fixed for the future.

That was it. I knew what he was thinking, and why. He was thinking of the two things that meant most to him. His given word, and me.

Was I worth it? Was I really worth all that? Was I worth any part of the hard work and suffering pa had gone through?

Was I?

CHAPTER 2

A moment there I sat very still . . . what *would* I do?

There had always been pa. Somehow I'd never had to worry because he was always there, telling me what to do. Time to time he got my dander up and I'd growl around for a few days, or I'd ride off to town to talk to Doc or the Kid, but when I got around to riding home, pa was always there.

Come to think of it, he had never held it up to me. Inside me there was a horrible, sinking feeling. Without pa, what was there? I'd be alone.

So far as I knew, I had no kinfolk anywheres at all, and the friends I had were pa's friends.

"Your ma," he said suddenly, "was a fine woman. I wish you could have knowed her. Educated, too. She came of good folks, and she had book learnin'.

"Her family was New England Irish . . . lace-curtain Irish. Time was I mentioned her family name to an Irishman and he says hers was an old family, born of the old chiefs of Ireland going back to before the Danes came."

Ma died when I was three and I remembered her only as somebody warm and wonderful who held me close and made much of me when I was hurt or feeling bad. She'd been a pretty woman. Pa said it, and that much I remembered. She died of a fever on Cache Creek when we was traveling to Texas.

It was sundown when we saw the fire, and it was far off. The country was no longer level, but broken into ravines, some of them choked with brush.

We forked out our rifles and closed in, but before we got within hailing distance we saw there were a couple of wagons and off to one side some mules picketed. It

23

was a camp of buffalo hunters.

One man taken one look at pa and said, "Mister, you better let me help you off that horse."

"My son will do it," pa said, and I helped him down, but as my hands took his weight I felt him tremble, and when I got him stretched out alongside the fire I looked into his eyes and saw that he was dying.

There was choking fear in me. I glanced around at their faces. "Is anybody here a doctor? Pa's in bad shape."

One man was already rolling his sleeves. "I ain't no saw-bones, but I'll see what I can do."

When he cut away pa's pants-leg I couldn't stand to look. The jagged end of the bone had come through the flesh and the wound looked ugly.

That man who'd said he was no doctor worked fast and he seemed to know exactly what to do.

Another man handed me a cup. "You're done up, boy. Have some coffee."

Whilst the man worked on pa and I ate and drank, I told them our story.

They were here," one of them said. "They pulled in last night and left shy of daylight. You aren't about to catch them."

"I got to. Pa taken them cows up the trail on trust, and the folks who trusted their cattle to him need their money."

There was a lean, well-set-up man with a reddish mustache who sat back from the fire.

He looked over at me. "My friend, you'd have to tie

into three men, and they'd be ready for you."

"Yes, sir," I said, "but they've got our money. I got to get it back."

"Do you know those men?"

So I explained about Doc and Reese and Heseltine, and how pa and me had words and I'd gone off and left him, and had I been there I could have caught that horse. Then I told about facing the three of them and backing down.

"You did right." The big bearded man who seemed to be the head man spoke emphatically. "I didn't cotton to that outfit myself. You'd have had no chance with the three of them . . . and your pa was waiting, his leg broken."

The man who had been treating pa walked over to me, rolling down his sleeves. "You'd better go sit by him, and you'd better stay with him. I think he'd like it."

Pa was resting quiet when I got to him. I could smell whiskey, and I guessed they had given it to him to ease the pain.

He caught hold of my hand. "Son, I never been much of a father. If your mother had lived I'd have done better. She had a feeling for things I never rightly had. Ever since your ma died I been trying to think out what she would have had me do with you. My own father was killed in a river accident when I was four."

"You done all right, pa. I just ain't much account."

"No, you're a good boy. You always were. I don't

25

hold it against you that you looked up to Doc Sites and Kid Reese. They must have seemed a lot more exciting than me."

"They couldn't hold a candle to you. Not even in their best days."

"I'd seen their like before." He looked at me. "When I was a boy, not much older than you, I traipsed around with some men not any better than Sites and Reese. I nigh got myself into more trouble than I could handle. I knew what could come of it."

He lay very still for a while and his breathing was slow and awful heavy. He seemed to have trouble catching his breath.

"I'm sorry for the folks at home," he said. "Teale wanted to send his girl to school, and Sackleton planned to buy a milk cow for his wife. Most of them needed money to tide them over until planting time. Now they'll be hard up."

"I'll get it back, pa. If it's the last thing I do."

"I wouldn't put it on you, son. You'll have to make your own way now.

He knew he wasn't going to make it. Right there he said it, and I sat there beside him, holding his hand, wishing I'd not said some of the mean things I'd said, wishing I'd listened more than I had, understood him better. I'd never stood in his boots, trying to make a living against the works of nature and the changes of money value and the like. I'd never had a boy to raise all alone.

"Pa," I whispered, not able to speak out loud, "pa,

I'll make it. I really will. I know what you tried to do for me, and I'll pay them back. You gave your word, and now I give you mine."

He kind of squeezed my hand, so I guess he heard me, and then he was dead. He went easy at the last, just a sort of sigh.

Gangrene had set in, the bearded man said, and the poison was all through him. They might have saved his life by taking off his leg, but nobody there had ever done the like, and anyway, he wouldn't hear of it.

We laid him to rest on a high knoll alongside the river, and I set up there with a cinch-ring held by two sticks and burned his name and the date into a wooden slab. Not that it would last long—things don't in that country. It was little enough mark for him to leave on the land. He lay there alone like many another before and after, simple men who just wanted to build their homes, and to help build a country.

If he was to make any mark at all it had to be through me. I was all he left in the world, aside from a worn-out saddle and a hard-used Winchester.

When I stuck that slab into the ground I went down the knoll to saddle up.

The man with the reddish mustache, he was standing there beside the fire, and he said, "You fixing to take in after those men?"

"Yes, sir. That's what pa would have done."

"Mind if I ride along? That's a lonely ride you've got ahead of you."

Well, I just looked at him and felt a lump come into

my throat. "Yes, sir. If you've a mind to."

"He was quite a man, that father of yours. Only death could stop a man like that."

"Death won't. I'm a-goin' to ride in his place."

"Were you very close? You and your pa?"

"No, sir. I wouldn't listen to him. I figured I was a whole sight smarter. I never guessed how much he knew."

"You aren't alone. A lot of us didn't listen when we should have. It takes time for a boy to appreciate his father."

He turned to the bearded man. "Wright, will you take my hides off my hands? And we'll need a couple of pack horses and some grub."

"All right, Con. Take what you've the need for."

And that was how I met Con Judy, and how we rode together on a trail that wasn't to see an end for a long, long time.

CHAPTER 3

The trail led toward the Canadian, and I learned a thing or two about Con Judy. Pa had been a good man on a trail, but he couldn't match up with Con. Time and again when I lost the trail he would pick it up, seeming to know almost by instinct the way they had taken.

Nobody talked less than he did, but you can learn about a man by riding with him. He never wasted a motion, never took an unnecessary chance. He scouted every possible ambush, every creek-crossing. He never made a point of it, but he knew what he was doing.

One day I told him what Doc and the Kid had said about Bob Heseltine. When I finished Con simply said, "You never know how a man will stack up until he's faced with it."

When pa died he left mighty little. He had eighteen dollars and a few cents in his pockets, and a worn-out pistol. His Winchester was better than mine. On the ranch we'd left behind there was a cabin, a corral, and a few head of scrub cattle alongside a water hole.

Eighteen dollars wasn't going to carry me far, but I had eight dollars of my own money and I could sell his pistol and my Winchester. They wouldn't bring much, but I'd get maybe fifteen to twenty dollars for them.

Toward sundown of the third day we rode up to Happy Jack's stage station. Whilst Con sat his horse, rifle in hand, I scouted the corral. None of the horses I was looking for was there.

Happy Jack came out, rolling down his sleeves. He had been washing up dishes after feeding the stage passengers. He didn't know me from Adam, but he knew Con Judy. I was to find that a lot of folks did.

"They were here," Happy Jack said. "Rode in about sundown last night. Bought themselves a meal and a couple of bottles and paid for it with gold money. I figure they're headed for Mobeetie or Dodge."

"They didn't say?"

"Nary a word."

So we set up to the table and finished the grub Jack had left from the stage crowd. It was venison steak and beans. Between the two of us we must have drunk a gallon of black coffee.

"That Heseltine," Jack suggested, "he had him a woman over to Granada. Worked in a saloon."

"Aren't many women in this country," Con Judy said.

"And he's got money," I added.

When we rode into Granada it was blowing a norther and it was cold. Made a body wonder what he'd done with his summer's wages.

Had the dust been just a mite thicker we could have gone right past the place without ever seeing the town.

There was a scattering of such towns over thousands of square miles—a half-dozen soddies, a saloon, and what passed for a store. There would be stacks of buffalo hides dried stiff as boards, corrals, and a lean-to that was both stable and blacksmith shop. Sometimes there was a creek, often just a seep of water or a spring. Occasionally there was a dug well.

The houses were unpainted, and grayed by wind and sun, street alternately muddy or dusty. This place was no better or no worse than any town beginning from nothing, struggling to make a shape and a plan for itself.

The man in the saloon said, "She's gone. Feller rode in here yestiddy. He done showed her some gold money and she lit out like her skirts was afire."

That was the way of it. We were always a little late, or a little too far behind.

We ate what the man had to offer, and neither of us did much talking. Finally Con said, "We might find a trail after this dust, but likely not. Heseltine has money and he has a girl, so I'm guessing he'll ride for some place where he can spend money. That means Denver City or Leadville."

We rode westward, and in the long silences of the prairie trail, with only the whisper of hoofs in the brown grass of autumn, my thoughts kept turning back to pa. It was little enough of a life he'd had, and I knew that the only way I could repay him was to trail those men down and take our money back to Texas. Pa had been a man to stand on principle, and I said as much to Con.

Con was older than me by ten years, I surmised, although he never said and folks in the West weren't much on asking or answering personal questions. A man was what he did, how he shaped up at work, or against trouble.

Con was hard to place. Mostly he spoke like an educated man, but other times he'd talk careless like those of us who didn't know any better. No two men can ride a trail together without coming to know each other, and I came to know Con Judy.

I found myself wanting to be like him. And after I'd been with him a while, I began to speak better—a little more the way he did.

He took to calling me Shell. That was after I told

him my right name was Edwin Shelvin Tucker.

"Shell," he said once, "the thing that shows the man is his willingness to accept responsibility for himself and his actions. Only a tinhorn blames what he is on his folks or the times or something else besides himself. There have been good men and great men in all periods of history, and they did it themselves."

The way he said things they never seemed like preaching, and even had they been, I'd have listened. Con Judy was the kind of man you believed. When I stacked Kid Reese and Doc Sites up against him, they came out the short-horns they were.

We found no more tracks and we looked for none. We were heading for Denver City, a fast-growing town with saloons and dance halls that were wide open to a man with money.

There was something nagging at me, and I mentioned it to Con. "That Heseltine now . . . I wonder how he'll like sharing that money with Sites and Reese? And even if he's willing, how about her?"

Con smiled. "You're growing up, Shell. I'd lay even money they've all done some thinking about that."

Never in my born days had I seen such a place as Denver. Brick blocks were going up all about, and several had been completed. The log cabins and sod houses that had been the beginning of the town looked down-at-heel and shabby beside the new buildings. Nor had I ever seen so many people. You'd have thought there was a picnic in town.

"How will we ever find them?" I asked Con. "I

never saw so many people before."

"We'll call on Jim Cook. He's been a lawman here, and he makes it his business to know all the crooks in the country and to keep them located. If they're here or have been here, he will know."

Jim Cook was a fine, tall man with a mustache. "Yes, I know the man. I believe he's in Leadville. There are more outlaws in that town today than any place in Colorado or Kansas."

We had camped in an arroyo. Con was making coffee and I had washed out my shirt and hung it on a bush to dry in the sun. Many a time I'd had to let the heat of my body dry a wet shirt, for a man couldn't pack much in the way of clothes when he was high-tailing it across country.

"After you catch up to them, what then?" Con asked me.

Con had a way of asking questions that set a man to thinking. Worrying, even.

Well, what would I do? Until now everything had been ordered by circumstances, or by pa. There had been work to do, and not much choice about when to do it.

If a man wanted to eat he had to work, and he had to be at it from sunup to sundown. I'd done a lot of day-dreaming, and a certain amount of that goes into the making of a man, but all that talk with Reese and Sites had been another kind of daydreaming.

Ofttimes a boy gets rid of some of the restlessness that's in him by imagining he's a wild *bandito* on the

Texas plains, and he thinks outlaws are bold and daring men. The trouble comes when he has to face up to reality, and then such daydreams had best be forgotten. There's something almighty real about a sheriff's posse, a loaded gun, and a hangman's noose.

What would I do? Get the money back, ride to Texas, and pay those folks what they had coming.

There'd be a little left, and there was the place. It was a good place, but it wasn't in me to go back there alone and raise cows.

Con said nothing more, but he surely didn't need to. He could ask questions a man found hard to answer, questions that made him face up to himself. When a man answered questions like that he found himself a lot wiser about himself and the world.

Like Con said one time, a man should stop ever' now and again and ask himself what he was doing, where he was going, and how he planned to get there. And the hardest thing to learn is that there aren't any shortcuts.

His questions nagged at me because whilst I had big ideas of what I wanted to do and become, I hadn't any way of making them into reality. I could imagine myself riding fine horses and wearing the best clothes, buying drinks in saloons, and maybe gambling a little for big stakes, but nowhere could I see where the money was coming from.

I said as much.

"Can you read?"

"Sure."

"Then read. Read anything, everything. You'll come up with an idea. But about the gambling for big stakes . . . forget it. That's just a way of showing off. If a man is something and somebody, he doesn't have to show off."

Come sunup, we were on the trail to Leadville.

The night we rode into the town there had been rain, and the clouds hung low among the mountains, right down over the store-tops, in fact, because Leadville was a high-up town. We'd had to stop again and again to let our horses get their breath.

The trail had been wet, and here the streets were muddy. Chestnut Street was empty when we slopped up the road between the rows of buildings. A horse was standing three-legged in the rain, bedraggled, woebegone, and miserable-looking.

We glimpsed a bookstore sign, and one for a Justice of the Peace, then Goldsoll's Loan Office, with a doctor's rooms upstairs.

We drew rein, sizing up the town, and looking for a saloon or a restaurant. Bob Heseltine and the others would be spending and gambling, and the sooner I could get our money back the more there would be to get.

Midnight was already long gone, but when we rounded a corner we saw some saloon lights shining through the rain, and beyond them a livery stable.

We put up our horses, walking through the place to see if any of the horses was familiar. The hostler watched us, his eyes gloomy. "Huntin' somebody?"

35

"Might be."

"They come, they go."

"Three men and a woman, a young woman . . . might be a dance-hall girl."

He studied us. "You'd not be wanting them. Not now."

"Why not now?"

"They've got friends. In this town you'd better have the right friends or you have nothing. And if you don't have the right friends all you'll have is enemies."

We walked up the street to a saloon and went up to the bar. Wet as it was, there were a good many men there.

The bartender started to place a bottle on the bar, then looked up and saw Con Judy. "Oh? Didn't recognize you, Mr. Judy."

He put the bottle away and got out a fresh one, a good brand of Scotch whiskey.

"Have you seen Bob Heseltine?"

"I saw him. He's over on State Street with a couple of friends and a girl . . . Ruby Shaw. She has friends over there . . . if you know what I mean."

Con filled our glasses. "Who's marshal now?"

"Mart Duggan. He's mean and dangerous, but he doesn't hunt trouble unless it hunts him . . . unless he's drinking."

"Ben . . . this is my partner, Shell Tucker. A favor to him is a favor to me."

Ben extended a hand. He was a medium-built man with sandy hair plastered down over a round head. He

36

had a quick, friendly way and a firm grip. "Ben Garry here. I've known Con for quite a spell."

We finished our drinks, and then pushed our way through the crowd, studying every face we saw. At the door Con stepped out first, and when I joined him, indicated the room we had left with a jerk of his head.

"They're all here, Shell. Rounders and drifters from every mining and cattle camp in the country. There's money to be made here and they can smell it. Ever do any mining, Shell?"

"No, sir. I'm pretty good with a pick and shovel, but no mining."

A lighted window showed a restaurant still open, and we crossed the street.

"There's beef," the man said, "and beans and potatoes. Might scare you up a piece of pie, but I ain't cookin' no more tonight. I'm done played out."

"It'll do . . . if there's coffee."

"There's a-plenty." He brought a fire-blackened pot to the table. "We fix a fair meal in the evenin', and there's breakfast, if'n I get up in time."

He put beef and beans on the table, and some slabs of homemade bread and butter. "Make our own butter. Have our own cows. We got us four Holsteins and we're buyin' more. Brung 'em over the trail m'self."

We ate in silence, but finally I asked a question that had been on my mind for days. "Do you think they know they're being followed?"

"I believe so."

"Then we might run into trouble when we don't expect it?"

"You must always expect it. When you start hunting men, they can hunt as well. Regardless of that, it pays to be on your toes. This town is rough, and the country is rough."

It was raining harder outside. If they were in Leadville the chances were slight they would attempt to leave in this storm. The trails were slippery and narrow, with always the danger of slides. Mountain country was new to me, and worrisome. There were too few trails and passes.

"The best trails are the Indian trails," Con advised. "Not many know of them. Indians traded back and forth across the country, traveling hundreds of miles . . . like the merchant caravans of the Middle Ages."

Now, I'd never heard about merchant caravans and wasn't exactly sure what he meant by the Middle Ages, so I kept my mouth shut and listened.

"Up in Minnesota they mine a soft red stone that is easily carved and smoothed. They call it pipestone. You will find that kind of stone among Indians all over the country.

"Shells, too. There are different types in different waters. Most of them are classified. Men have devoted years to studying the various types of shells."

Con Judy, who rarely talked more than two or three sentences at a time, told me then of the trade trails left by ancient Indians.

"Ancient Indians? You mean different from the ones here now?"

"Yes. Just as we have pushed them back, they pushed others before them. It's happened all the way across the world, Shell, and you'll see it happening right here."

"Then the best fighters end up by owning the country?"

He chuckled. "Not exactly, Shell. Let's put it this way: the ones who wind up on top are usually those with the most efficient lifestyle."

Just what he meant by that I wasn't sure, but before I could ask him he said, "We'd better get some sleep," and pushed back from the table.

"And then I've got to find Heseltine," I said. "It isn't likely they'll be traveling on a night like this, not with a girl, and all."

"They'll hole up," Con agreed.

He paid for our meal and we started for the door. I was studying about what he meant by lifestyle, and I had just pushed open the door when I remembered my Winchester. I'd left it lying across the table next to ours.

Turning sharply, I bumped Con hard and we both staggered and almost fell.

But we both heard the gun and we heard the bullet strike.

Had I not turned just as I did, I'd have been a dead man.

CHAPTER 4

Behind us a light went out, then another, and there was darkness. Neither of us moved. I was on one knee just inside the door, my heart pounding.

Scared? Well, I should reckon. It taken some time to get used to the idea that I'd been shot at. A body thinks of such things, but thinking isn't like the real thing. Somebody out there had shot, and shot to kill, and he'd been shooting at me.

That takes some getting used to. In all that gunplay I'd practiced and all the gun battles I'd played out in my mind, there'd been nothing like this. That man out there was trying to *kill* me!

Kid Reese? Doc Sites? Or was it Heseltine? "Stay right where you are, Shell," Con warned.

You want to know something? I wasn't figuring on going no place a-tall.

Turning my head ever so slightly, I could see what he meant. The light from the window next door fell across the room, and anybody moving would surely be seen. Whoever had done that shooting was good.

So we just set still while the moments passed. It seemed a long time. My heart slowed down after a bit, and my hand got so sweaty on my gun butt that I moved to wipe it off on my britches.

"Give him time, Shell. Whoever he is, he's standing in the rain yonder between the buildings. He'll get tired of it before we will."

"I ain't movin'," I said. "I'm fixin' to spend the night—only that gent over there don't know that."

"You ever been shot at before, Shell?"

"No, sir. Not really. Had some Injuns one time who cut loose at the house. They were shootin', all right, but not at nobody in pa'ticular. That gent yonder was mighty pa'ticular, I'm thinking."

So we waited. My rifle was close by, but I hesitated to reach for it, although I doubted if it was where it could be seen.

"Crawl around close to the wall, then through the kitchen door. I'll cover you."

After I started to crawl I could reach my rifle, so I latched onto it, and when I got into the kitchen I stood up in the dark doorway and looked out at the rain-sodden street. I could see nothing but the slanting rain across the window.

Con crawled the other way and joined me.

We heard the cook stirring, saw the glow of his cigar. "You boys always pack trouble with you? Or is this here somethin' new?"

"You got a back door?"

"Yonder. . . . If you boys was figurin' on havin' breakfast, there's a good restaurant on the other side of town."

"You'll never get rich sendin' business away," I said. "We like your place."

"I might not get rich," he said dryly, "but I'll live a lot longer. Well, come back if you've a mind to. On'y, if you boys don't mind I'll stand my ol' Sharps along-side the door. If anybody shoots into my kitchen I'm goin' to shoot back."

"You don't sound like a restaurant man," Con Judy commented.

"Hell, I cooked for m'self nigh onto twenty year, an' for cow camps and the like. Seemed to me it was a sight easier than sweatin' it out down in one of those mines."

At the back door we waited a minute and studied the layout. I reckoned the risk was mine so I stepped out first. But I'll own to it . . . I was scared.

Con Judy followed and we slopped down the alley, circled back of a couple of buildings and went to the livery barn. We didn't want to go hunting a place to sleep when the very place we found might be where our enemies had holed up, so we got our bedrolls and crawled into the haymow.

When we stretched out Con said, "Do you still have it in mind to hunt those boys down?"

"I got it to do," I replied. "I'm not anxious to get my head blowed off, but pa surely would have hung on, was it him. I can't do any less."

"They'll have divided it up by now."

"Maybe. But you got to think about that girl. She won't want any divvying done, if she can help it. She won't want to see all that money getting away."

Another thing worried me. The jingle of money in my jeans was a disappearing sound. Those few dollars were about gone, even with riding the grub line part of the way, and spending careful. Leadville was a town where folks lived high, and money wouldn't last long. I had no idea how Con was fixed, but it was enough that he shared trouble with me, without carrying the load of feeding both of us as well.

Lying there, hands behind my head, staring up into the dark and listening to the rain on the roof, I studied the situation I was in.

In most places there was no law that extended beyond the limits of a town, although county governments had been formed here and there where they had a sheriff who would chase criminals if he felt like it. Jim Cook was, according to Con, making an effort to get marshals and sheriffs to work together against the bad ones.

But when it came right down to it I had no legal case against anybody. They had found a lost horse, and even if two of them knew who the horse belonged to they could deny it, and I hadn't any proof the horse and money was mine.

What lay between us was a simple matter of justice, and I was in no mood to let them steal the money of hard-working folks who trusted us. Nor mine either, when it came to that.

Pa was dead, and had it not been for my fool bull-headedness and their stealing, he might still be alive.

Yet I did not want to get killed, and that bullet into the doorjamb showed me they knew we were on their trail, and they were ready for us. I studied about it, but came to no good conclusion. Of course I was scared, but it wasn't in me to quit. Well, maybe it was . . . but not yet.

Toward the end, before I fell asleep, I got to thinking about Con Judy.

Why had he come with me? To see that I didn't get my head blown off? Because he was ready to drift, anyway? Because he didn't like to see injustice done? Here I was riding partner with a man I hadn't known at all. About all I knew about him now was that I figured he had more education than I'd ever have. But I was learning things from him.

When morning came and I was brushing off the hay I'd picked up during the night in the loft, I laid it out for Con. "I want that money back. I'm not vengeful, but I aim to get it."

Putting on my hat, I added, "I'm surely going to have to get it quick, or rustle some work. I've only got a little money left."

"How do you figure to get it?"

"First off, I'm simply going to them and ask for it."

Con made no reply until he had tugged on his boots. He got up and stamped them into place on his feet. "That is about as simple a method as anybody could suggest. And when they refuse, as they surely will, what then?"

"I'll tell everybody in town what happened."

"They may say you're just crying. In this country a man fights his own battles."

"You're surely right, but I'm beginning to find out there's a whole lot they don't know. Pa was forever trying to tell me things, but I wouldn't listen. I thought pa was a stick-in-the-mud, and Doc and the Kid knew more than he did."

Belting on my six-shooter, I took up the Winchester. "What I figure is this. I want folks to know where I stand. I want folks to know why I am after those three, and just what they've done . . ."

"Do you think that will help?"

"I just ain't sure. But if it comes to a shooting affair and I kill one of them, I want folks to know I'm not just a murderer."

He nodded. "That's good thinking. But if you tell that story around, one of them is sure to call you a liar."

"And there'll be shooting? Is that what you mean?"

We climbed down the ladder from the loft and studied the layout. Neither of us wanted to be dry-gulched. "When you tell that story," Con said, "wear your gun loose. You'll surely need it."

We started off to get breakfast. "Have you ever been in a gun battle?"

"No, sir."

"Then don't try a fast draw. You'll get yourself killed. Take your time, get your gun out, and make the first shot count . . . you may not get another."

"I'm pretty fast."

"Forget it. You've no idea whether you're fast or not, and the only way you'll find out is against some-body. If you're wrong, you're dead.

"Anyway, most of the fast draws I've seen ended

with the first shot going into the dust right out between the two of them. So take your time, and make your first one good. If your man goes down, or staggers, continue to shoot. But slowly . . . and carefully."

After a moment he added, "I've seen men kill with half a dozen bullets in them. Don't count a man as dead until you've seen them fill in his grave."

There seemed to be nobody watching the restaurant. A good many people were coming and going along the street, and some rigs were tied here and there, or were passing. The street was chewed up and muddy. The clouds had broken and a ray of sunshine was bright on the face of the restaurant.

We crossed the street, pausing once to let a freight wagon pass, drawn by half a dozen bulls. On the boardwalk we stamped the mud from our feet. My eyes happened to go up and I caught a flicker of movement at a curtained window.

"Somebody up there. First window over the hardware store."

"All right," Con said, "let's go inside."

The man who had served us the night before was on the job. He was a hard-bitten old man with gnarled hands that looked as if they'd spent years wrapped around a pick handle.

"I got the Sharps," he commented. "I don't take kindly to folks shootin' into my place of business."

"Ought to be a law against it," I said.

He didn't wait to take our order. He just brought out a big stack of flapjacks and a pitcher of syrup and set them on the table. "I got eggs and meat if you want them."

"I'll stick with flapjacks," I said. "I got me an eggs-and-meat appetite, but a flapjack bankroll."

"Eat up. If a man's going to get shot coming out of my restaurant I want folks to figure he ate well, anyhow."

We ate. The meat was venison, fresh shot in the mountains. The eggs were fresh laid—sometime or other.

The man was a talker, like many lonely men I've known. They herd sheep or cattle, or prospect by themselves, and when they come into town they talk, just to hear the sound of their own voice and some-body answering.

He told us about Leadville. It hadn't had the name for long, and actually, he said, there was more silver than lead. The town had been Oro City for a while, and before that it was Slabtown. Back around 1860 a man named Abe Lee had done some placer mining in California Gulch.

The town never amounted to much until a prospector took on a partner who told him that reddish sand he'd been throwing out was carbonate of lead, with a silver content so high it scared him. Business picked up, and the town boomed.

Presently the man brought a fresh pot of coffee to the table and sat down with us.

"We're ten thousand feet up," he said, "and she gets awful cold. Folks around here say we get ten months

47

of winter, and two months mighty late in the fall."

Mountains reared up all around the town, with the trees playing out at timberline. The mountains were scarred with prospect holes; everybody was mining, everybody dreaming about making the big strike. Those who weren't actually digging had grub-staked men who were. The idea of getting rich was in the air.

There'd been only a scattering of folks along the creeks at first, but now there was somewhere between thirty and sixty thousand people, depending on who you talked to and how sober he was. The men who were making money spent it; they drank champagne like water. Men who didn't even care for champagne drank it because a man who had money spent it, and champagne was the mark of riches.

Con told me that a good deal of what passed for champagne was made in a building off an alley down the street. They had some youngsters running around picking up the empty bottles and refilling them.

One Irish laborer struck it rich and went down the street buying suits for everybody he knew. He didn't know me and I was kind of slow getting acquainted. By the time I could call him by name his pocket had played out and he was putting the bum on me for a meal. My luck ran that way . . . and well out in front of me.

I wasn't likely to be one of the nabobs who ate at the Tontine. I was lucky to get a plate of oxtail soup at Smoothey's, which sold for five cents and was in my class of income.

Con and me, hunting them, ran into Doc Sites and Kid Reese at the Bon Ton. We were pushing through the crowd and came face to face with them.

"Hello, Kid," I said. "You and Doc getting ready to return my money?"

Several people stopped to listen, smelling excitement, and the Kid's face kind of thinned down. He threw a quick look at Doc, but Doc was looking at me.

"What're you talkin' about?" the Kid blustered.

"You took pa's horse with our money on it, and money that belonged to a lot of poor folks down in Texas. You knew that horse was ours. I'd loaned it to you a time or two."

The Kid started to push by, because more people were stopping to listen. "That ain't so!" he said roughly.

Then I opened my big mouth and said the one thing I shouldn't have, "You callin' me a liar, Kid?"

All of a sudden we weren't crowded any more. There was space all around us.

The Kid stood stock-still, his face white and stiff, and Doc was off to one side, as if he had no part in it.

I'd had no idea of throwing a challenge at him like that. It just sort of came out.

"I ain't called you nothin'," he said, and shoved by me. I let him go.

Doc started to leave too. "Doc," I said, "I want my money. You and the Kid bring it to the Jolly Cork eatin' house, and have it there by noontime."

Doc never said a word. He just pushed by and went

out, and folks started talking again. One man offered to buy us a drink. "What was that all about?" he asked.

So I told him.

"He may come a-shootin'," he said when I'd finished.

"Yes, sir. I reckoned on that, but I can't see my way clear to gettin' my money unless I carry trouble to them."

The man thrust out a hand. "I'm Bill Bush. I like the way you stand, so if you need a friend, call on me."

"Yes, sir. If you know where a man could get a few days of work, I'd be obliged. Chasing these men has run me short."

Con Judy stepped up then, and Bush saw him for the first time. "Howdy, Con. I didn't recognize you there at first. Do you know this man?"

"We're riding together."

I'd heard tell of Bill Bush. He was partners with Silver Dollar Tabor, one of the most prominent men in town, and occasionally his rival.

"I didn't know you were in this part of the country, Con."

"Tried my hand at buffalo hunting. When Shell Tucker came along, I threw in with him."

"You've got some old friends in town, Con. Dave May[1] has opened a department store here—I think you knew him. Meyer Guggenheim[2] has a share in some mining properties, and there's talk of building a smelter."

Bush finished his drink. "Why don't you fellows

join me for dinner at the Tontine? I'd appreciate it."

"Thanks," I said, "but I—"

"We'll come," Con interrupted. "About seven?"

Outside, I said, "Con, you know I ain't fixed to go such a place. My clothes aren't fit, and besides, pa always said a man should have the money to carry his share of the load, and I ain't got it."

"Don't worry. I want you to come. As for the clothes, we can buy you an outfit. When you get some money you can pay me back."

"You got it to spare? Con, I wouldn't want to put you in a bind."

"My credit is good."

With Con to advise, I bought a black suit, some shirts, underwear, ties, and what-all. It was more clothes than I'd ever had at one time in my life. He suggested I also buy some new riding clothes, so I did.

Leaving May's store, we walked around to the Clarendon Hotel, completed only a short time before. That and the Grand, operated by Thomas Walsh[3] were the places to stay. I'd never been inside such a place before, but when Con Judy walked up to the desk you'd have thought he owned the place.

Nothing was said about money, and if anybody thought we were dressed rough for the hotel they made no comment. Leadville was used to men in digging clothes who turned into millionaires overnight.

Upstairs in our room, Con motioned toward the bath. "You first," he said. "I've got to see some people."

Well, that bath was mighty fine. When I'd finished and I'd shaved, I dolled up in that black suit, and looked to be worth as much as any man in the place.

Con came back, glanced at me, and nodded. "You'll do, Shell. Better stay in the room—I'll be ready in a jiffy."

I didn't have any plans for going out. I wasn't anxious to get shot up in my new suit, but I was wishing I could get the crease out of my store-bought suit before I went where folks could see me. That crease was a sure sign my suit had come off the shelf, and wasn't tailored. Nobody had creases in their pants if they could help it.

When Con came back into the room he was dressed and ready. He'd left an outfit at the hotel some months earlier.

When we entered the Tontine half an hour later anybody would have taken us for a couple of swells. Nobody would have guessed I was a poor boy off the cap rock of Texas. But in my waistband I was packing a gun.

I was ready. I was real ready.

CHAPTER 5

The Tontine was the most elegant place I'd ever been in, and as I sat quiet at the table listening to the talk between Bill Bush, who owned the Clarendon, and Con Judy, I began to see that those outlaws I'd thought so important were really a mighty small catch.

Con smoked a long black Cuban cigar and talked about railroads, hotels, and banking until I couldn't believe he was the same man I'd met in a buffalo camp.

The thing that surprised me was how everybody listened to what he had to say. I mean, you felt he was somebody important. During supper half a dozen men stopped by to speak to him, and to ask his opinion on this or that.

Of course, as pa had told me and as I'd learned of my ownself, you never knew who you were meeting around a campfire, in a bunkhouse or a saloon. Men took on the color of the country they were in, assumed its ways of speaking, its dress and manners.

From what was said I gathered that Con was an engineer, that he'd speculated in mines, railroads, and steamboats, and had made half a dozen fortunes.

He was respected. Bill Bush and David May, who everybody said was an up-and-coming man, listened with attention to what Con said.

"You should go into road-building, Con," Bush said. "Colorado has the ore, but we need roads to get it out. The best mines are in the high country, and to many of the mines there are only trails."

Bush left us to talk to some friends, and Con talked to me about some of the men we'd met. He pointed out a man across the room. "He's got a nice business now, and he's going to make it big." Con brushed the ash from his cigar. "When he came into town he was broke. He found out they were refilling champagne bottles, so he began collecting them. They say he collected over nine thousand, saved his money, and started trading."

Several of the men who stopped by the table had heard that somebody had taken a shot at Con, and he corrected them and told them it was me who had been shot at. Shooting was no unusual thing in Leadville, but it didn't happen every day, either, and nobody likes a dry-gulcher who'll shoot out of the dark at a man.

When we were alone, Con said, "Shell, you'll find times when you have to fight. The secret is never to hunt trouble."

"You mean I shouldn't look for Reese and them?"

"I did not say that. They brought trouble to you. The money is rightfully yours, and you must settle it as you see fit.

"I brought you here tonight for several reasons. First, because you are my friend and I enjoy your company. Second, because I wanted some of the respectable citizens of the town to know you in case there is trouble later. Third, because it is time for you to realize there are other aspects of the world than those you have seen so far."

He paused, drank some coffee, and then went on, "We will always have Reeses and Heseltines, and they will always seem big and brave to growing boys. They swagger and make loud noises in their own little circle, but they are only the coyotes that yap around the heels of the herd.

"Remember this, Shell, the coyotes aren't going anywhere, but the herd is, and so are the men who drive the herd."

There was sense in what he said, but it rankled a little bit. I didn't like the feeling that I hadn't known better, but it was true that in this place a man like Reese would have been pretty small potatoes.

"Guns don't count in this place," Con continued. "Here it is intelligence, energy, the ability to begin and complete a job. Those are the things that matter."

He waved a hand around the room. "Some of them will make it big, some will fail, but all are trying. They are making money, but they are building a nation in the process. They will make mistakes . . . one always does when one moves fast, but they will accomplish a great deal, too. When a man opens a mine, builds a mill or a railroad, he has not only done something for himself but he has opened a way for others to make a living, many of whom he will never know or see; often they will live far from him or what he has done.

"We won't have a perfect country until we have perfect people, but we can try."

"That's all well enough, Con, but I've got to get my money back. Will they help me?"

He smiled. "No. Everybody rides his own broncs, Shell, and well you know it. They won't help you because that's your business, but they will be watching to see how you do it, and how you do it will

55

be remembered. And there is something else. If you handle this in a straight-forward manner, you'll have all their weight behind you when the shooting is over . . . and it can make a difference.

"If a stranger, a drifting cowhand, comes into town and shoots somebody he may get pretty rough handling before anybody knows the why of it. Western men are inclined to be abrupt. So now they know about you. They know your story and what you'll be doing.

"There's one other man I want you to meet," Con added, "but he doesn't often come here. Tonight he has. I heard he would be coming here tonight; once several years ago I helped him out of a tight corner."

A man loomed up over the table, and I looked up. He was a big man, with hard, red-rimmed eyes. He was unshaven and he was dressed roughly, with food stains on his coat and vest. He wore a gun and a badge.

"Mart Duggan . . . Shell Tucker."

He stared at me, and I felt uncomfortable under those hot, rather cruel-looking eyes. "Howdy," he said briefly. "Heard about you," he added. "Round 'em up if you're of a mind to—you'll have no trouble from me."

He glanced over at Con and a slow smile warmed his face. "Good to see you, Judy. If this man is a friend of yours, he's a friend of mine."

Turning abruptly, he walked across to the door and left.

"Mart Duggan," Con said, "is the law in Leadville at the moment. He's about as friendly as a grizzly bear with a sore tooth. He'll shoot a man as quick as look at him, and he doesn't seem to be afraid of anything on earth."

"He won't help me either?"

"No. But now he will stay off your back while you're settling your affairs."

I stood up. It began to look as if I had it to do. I was all jumpy inside, and my mouth was dry, but it was all laid out for me. In this country a man did what he had to do, and if he wasn't big enough for the job, he could always figure on a nice funeral if he died game.

"I'm going back to the Clarendon," I said, "and change clothes. Then I'm going to hunt until I find them."

Con Judy got up, too. "We'll both look," he said. "I wouldn't want you to face all three of them alone."

State Street was where the gamblers and the shady ladies were. The Little Casino, the Odeon, the Bucket of Blood, the Bon Ton, and the Pioneer—we made them all.

We ran into Minnie Purdy, Frankie Page, and Sallie Purple, some of the town's leading madams, and we saw Soapy Smith, Charlie Tanner, and Broken-Nose Scotty, all well known around town. But we saw neither hide nor hair of Reese, Sites, or Heseltine.

At Madame Vestal's place on State Street we took a table where we could watch the dancing. When the madame saw Con she walked over.

"How are you, Con? Are you going to stay around long?"

"That depends, Belle. Sit down, won't you?"

She sat down and looked over at me. "You'll be Shell Tucker. I've heard about you."

"Me?"

"By this time," Con Judy replied, "everybody in town has. When you're looking for a man or men the story doesn't take long . . . especially on State Street."

"Bob Heseltine is a bad man, Tucker," she said. "If I were you I'd forget it."

Well, I just looked at her for a moment, and then I said, "Thank you, ma'am, but I have it to do."

She studied me for a moment. "I like you, Tucker, and you have a good friend here in Con. I'll tell you this: Ruby Shaw was always friendly to Minnie Purdy."

"Thank you, ma'am," I said, and she moved on.

Con watched her go, thoughtfully. "There's a strange woman, Shell. Here they call her Madame Vestal, but once she was a mighty important woman, important in society, and even more important during the war."

"Her?"

"She was Belle Siddons then, a noted spy, and a daring young woman."

Pa used to tell stories about her. I remembered them now, and looked after her, wondering. These last few days I'd met some people mighty different from any I'd ever met before, different in many ways. And

Belle Siddons, or Madame Vestal or whatever her name was, had been helpful.

Minnie Purdy might know where Ruby Shaw was—the woman with Bob Heseltine—and where Ruby would be, there'd be Bob Heseltine close by. I had my lead, my first good one.

"She won't be likely to tell you anything, Shell," Con said.

I shrugged. "Didn't figure on it, but maybe if I keep my mouth shut and sort of scout around I can locate some sign."

So whilst Con Judy picked up with old acquaintances, I sat by and studied about Heseltine and the others. First off, they knew I was in town, for they'd shot at me. Having tried once, they would surely try again. That I had to take into account. All the time I was hunting them, they'd be hunting me.

Now you might think, in a town no bigger than Leadville, that it would be easy to find somebody, but as a matter of fact there were all those dives along State Street, and a lot of shacks and cabins around, and there were half a dozen clusters of buildings round about Leadville, each with its own name, and they might be holed up in any one of them.

There was Tintown, Jacktown, Little Chicago, Malta, Finntown, and a dozen other places along the valley of the Arkansas, up Stray Horse Gulch or Evans Gulch. A man who wanted to stay hid could do it.

Would they all hole up in the same place? It was likely.

At the same time there's gossip. With all the comers and goers in a boom town like Leadville, there's talk, and Ruby Shaw was a pretty woman, by most accounts, and pretty women are hard to keep out of sight.

It would be easier if it wasn't for all those little communities around. There was no way a man could watch them all. But I had an idea that folks with money on their hands weren't anxious to stay holed up. Nor did they worry much about me.

What they were running from more than from me was simply the knowledge they'd done wrong, and not wanting to be faced with it. Con Judy had done me a favor, too, by introducing me to the big men around town . . . that was going to worry them some.

Their horses . . . it was easier for a man to hide himself than to hide his horse. They'd have to keep their horses close to hand, and the horses would have to be fed.

We went back to the Clarendon, and you can bet I kept an eye out for trouble, but there was none.

And then I had one of those breaks that come to a man if he's keeping his eyes and ears open.

The lobby of the Clarendon had half a dozen people in it, and smelled of cigar smoke. Sitting on a leather settee was a man smoking a cigar and reading a newspaper.

There were a couple of others talking and sharing a brass spitoon. Con Judy had gone upstairs to get some papers he wanted to discuss with a man in the lobby and I was just sort of idling about. All of a sudden a girl came out of the restaurant and crossed the lobby. She was a few years older than me, and blonde, maybe a little hard around the mouth and eyes, but a fine figure of a girl.

The man with the newspaper stood up suddenly and said, "Ruby Shaw! How nice to see you here! Why, the last time I saw you was in Fort Worth."

They stood talking for a minute, and then she went out. Ruby Shaw . . .

I wasn't more than a moment getting to the door. She was down the street, almost to the corner. It looked as if she'd stopped to glance at a sign, because just then she started moving again, and I followed.

She never looked back even once, but when I glanced around I saw the man she had spoken to standing in the door looking after us.

For three blocks I followed her, moving carefully from door to door, and when she turned another corner I was only a few steps behind her. At the corner I stopped, close against the buildings, and looked after her.

She paused in front of a building, looking up and down the street, and then she turned and entered a doorway.

For a moment I stood there, studying the street and the building. It was two stories high, with a balcony along the front, and several windows as well as two doors on the ground floor. One of the doors, the one she had entered, I thought probably led to the upstairs.

Nobody else seemed to be on the street. It was still muddy from the rain but I could see a few dry spots where a man might cross without getting his boots too muddy. I did not want them caked with mud, for mud crunches underfoot and makes one's movements too loud.

No light showed upstairs, though maybe there was one in back. I walked down the block to get a look at the back of the building. There was a dim light in one room on the upper floor.

Who was up there? Ruby Shaw was Heseltine's girl, and Reese as well as Sites might be somewhere else. But Heseltine would have a part of my money.

My mouth was pretty dry as I walked toward the front again. I did not want to open that dark door, climb the stairs inside, and go along a dark hall to that lighted room. Every foot of it would be a danger, and then I'd have to knock on the door. I couldn't just open it, there being a woman in there—she might be undressing. The thought of it almost stopped me. I didn't want to run into any shameful things, or embarrass an undressing woman . . . or myself.

Yet I had to go ahead.

Slipping the thong off my gun-hammer, I went softly along the boardwalk and opened the door with my left hand. It opened out slowly . . . all was dark inside.

This was something new for me, and I did not want to get myself killed, and as pa always warned me, "If you go among the Indians you have to think like them." Stepping through the door, I found myself in a narrow hall. On my left was a door that might lead to a storeroom or cellar. A stairway went up to the rooms on the second floor.

Walking along the hall toward the back, I found myself facing a door, invisible except for the white porcelain knob. On my left was the newel post at the foot of the stairway. Putting my left hand on the post, I went around it to the first step.

Something was on my foot . . . mud dropped by the girl, no doubt. Pausing, I scraped my instep off against the edge of the stair, then started up.

I'd taken two steps when that door behind me opened. I turned, my left hand going to the wall as I sank to a crouch on the steps, my right hand coming up with my gun even as a shotgun belched a twin bore of flame. The thundering roar in the narrow hall drowned the two shots from my pistol.

There was a moment when I crouched in stunned silence. Scraping my foot had saved my life, for he had been counting my steps and believed I was one step higher. He had aimed for my waistline and had missed me by a foot or more.

It was only a split second that I was still, then I went up the steps two at a time. A door was opening a crack; it was not quite dark inside.

My shoulder hit the door and smashed it open; somebody fell to the floor with a crash.

By a dim reflected light in the room I could see a bed topped with a gray blanket, the brass bedstead gleaming dully, a dresser with a white bowl and pitcher. Stepping back, I held my gun on the fallen man and said quietly, "Get up slowly and light a light. I can see you well enough to shoot, and I've just killed one man."

Whether that was true or not, I did not know, but I figured to see where I was and who I was with.

"Don't shoot! For God's sake, don't shoot!"

Slowly the man got up, struck a match, and lit the kerosene lamp. Then he turned to face me . . . a perfect stranger.

"Mister," I said, "I'd no right to bust in. I was hunting Kid Reese, Bob Heseltine, and them."

"They pulled their freight," he said. "Heseltine, the girl, and another gent. One of them was layin' for you."

"You knew that?"

"Heard talk." He jerked his head toward the wall. "Nobody builds walls thick enough these days. I heard some talk, but I'd no idea what it meant. Then when the girl come up the steps, I seen her. Right off, she and two others left."

"How?"

"Yonder." He indicated the balcony. "A feller can step from this balcony to the next one pretty easy. There's a stairway down."

I took up the lamp and went down the stairs. I could hear voices, and folks coming along the street.

The dead man lay sprawled at the foot of the steps— only he wasn't dead. I'd put two bullets in him, all right, but he was alive and staring up at me.

"Doc," I said, and I still held the gun, "I want my money."

"They . . . they got it."

"You're not carrying any of it?" I kicked the shotgun and bent over him.

Just then the door opened and Duggan came in. Con Judy was with him.

"I think this man is carrying some of my money," I said.

"Take it off him then," Duggan said. Looking down at Doc Sites he said, "You shot high, boy. You got to watch that."

"It was in the dark, and when he came out of that door I dropped on the steps. He'd counted wrong and figured I was one step higher."

Opening Sites's coat, I saw a thick money-belt and took it from him. Sites lay still, staring at me. "Help me!" he said hoarsely. "I'm dying."

"My pa died," I said, "because of you and them."

Duggan was sizing up the situation. Doc Sites's position, the place where the double charge of buck-shot had hit the step and my own bullet holes in Sites made it clear enough.

The man into whose room I had burst came down the steps, slipping his suspenders over his shoulders. They'd been hanging loose when I had him light the lamp.

"It's like this here man says," he told them. "I was fixin' for bed when I heard all this sudden scurryin' about and seen them take off across the balcony.

"Somebody—it must've been the wounded man—went down the steps in the dark an' I heard the door close at the foot of the steps. Now that there is an empty room, and it didn't seem right, somehow, a man goin' into an empty room in the dark.

"Then I heard this man, comin' cautious-like. I opened the door for a peek, then closed it. Heard the shots and opened it again."

The smell of gunpowder hung in the narrow hall. Sites still stared up at us. "You goin' to let me die?"

"Serve you right," Duggan said, "but I'll see you're fetched."

I showed him the money-belt. "I'm taking this along," I said. "It's part of my money."

Duggan shrugged. "Lucky to get yourself part of it, but was I you I'd take after those others."

Back at the Clarendon I opened the money-belt and counted out the gold. One hundred pieces—one hundred twenty-dollar gold pieces, but it was only a small part of what I had lost.

"Either they haven't divided it up even," I said, "or they have and Doc cached most of his share."

"We'd better search his room," Con said thoughtfully, and right away, before somebody else does."

"Con," I said, "I don't believe we'll find it."

He studied me, then he smiled. "You're learning, Shell. You think the others took it along?"

"Figure it out for yourself. From what I know of them I'd say they'd steal from each other as quick as from me and pa. Doc was going to lay for me with a shotgun. They figured he'd get me, but in case he didn't—"

"And if he did? And found his money gone?"

"They'd give it back. He wouldn't dare brace Bob Heseltine and call him a thief. They'd just say they took care of it for him."

"So what are you going to do?"

I shrugged. "Sleep. In the morning I'm going to put most of this in the bank. I'm going to keep two hundred dollars as part of my share and use it to live on whilst tracking them down."

Before I went to sleep I sat down, and taking some paper the hotel provided, I struggled through the writing of a letter. I addressed it to Burton J. Ely, who was our neighbor, and who'd had a share in the herd.

CHAPTER 6

By noontime everybody in Leadville seemed to have heard about the shooting. Doc Sites was alive and might remain so, and I hoped he would. I had no need in me to kill Doc Sites, despite the fact he'd laid for me with a shotgun.

Because I had dropped on the steps, my shots had gone high, and his double charge had gone right past my head, a little high and to the right. At that close range the shots hadn't begun to scatter, but they blew a hole in the step you could put a fist through.

At breakfast men stopped by the table where I sat with Con Judy. "Served him right," they said. One added, "Only next time make it a mite lower. We don't need his kind."

We heard nothing of Heseltine or Reese. It seemed likely they had pulled their freight. Con had business in town so I nosed about, keeping the thong off my six-shooter just in case.

Con cautioned me, "Let them run and hide. Ruby won't like that, and we both know it. Money's no good unless they can spend it, and she will get tired of being holed up with two jumpy outlaws."

"What I can't figure," I said, "is why they're so scared. Heseltine is surely better than me with a pistol, and for that matter, Reese must be too."

Con shrugged. "When they knew you back in Texas you were just a shave-tail kid, and when they braced you back on the trail you weren't much more. They had only contempt for you, Shell. Men will often take advantage of anyone they believe is helpless to retaliate.

"The change in their thinking started when you took after them. That worried them, because it showed you weren't afraid to meet them. They probably didn't know who I was, and they were worried because you were no longer alone.

"Despite all the talk you hear about gunmen, most of them stay in their own district and avoid people on the other side of town. When you came to Leadville you seemed to have connections, and that would worry them. You can bet they heard talk; they knew you had cleared yourself with Duggan, and you seemed to be friendly with businessmen around town. You were no longer somebody to be treated with contempt.

"Then after somebody took that shot at you, that put them in the wrong. It was a shot from the dark—and it was a damn fool thing to do because it put them on record for the kind of men who would dry-gulch a man, and it also showed they weren't sure of their own position."

It made sense, of course. Nevertheless, I was worried about that money. If they had hit the trail I might never get any more of it, and I didn't like the thought of that. Anyway, town was a-fretting me.

I'd been raised where the long wind blows and the short-grass plains roll away to the edge of the sky. I was used to the smell of a buffalo-chip fire and the feel of a saddle. I'd had it in me too long to get quickly weaned away by fancy grub and store-bought clothes.

So I said nothing, but laid in a stock of traveling grub and a couple hundred rounds of .44's that would fit either my Winchester or my hand gun.

"You figurin' on startin' a war?" the man there in the hardware store asked me.

"Well, sir," I said, "those men taken money we'd been paid for cattle gathered by pa and his neighbors. Those folks sweat hard for that money. They made their gather in rain or shine or hail, and they held those cattle, come storm or stampede. Those folks back yonder trusted us. I figure if it has to be a war, it'll be a war."

He reached under the counter and come up with a six-shooter. It was mighty close to being new, and it was a fine weapon, fine as a man could wish.

"Boy," he said, "that gun you're packin' looks mighty used up, and I like the way you shape up. You take this here gun in place of the one you've got, and welcome."

"I can't afford it."

"Maybe. But I can. If you get your money, you ride by here and pay me; if you don't, forget it. I wouldn't want to see a man go up against Bob Heseltine with a wore-out gun."

"Thanks," was all I could say.

That gun had a feel to it, the right kind of feel. I held it in my hands and felt the balance of it, and I tried it in my holster and they fit as if they were made for each other.

"That's a fine piece," I commented, "and it's had some use. Is it yours?"

"My brother carried that gun. He was a good man, but the morning he was killed he wasn't carrying it, but an old one he was takin' to be fixed."

"What happened?"

"He'd had words with a man, a good time back. He met the man on the street, and my brother was killed. We buried him two years ago outside of Tin-Cup."

"Sorry."

"He knew that man was huntin' him. He bought this

gun for the purpose, and he had used it some. He loved the gun, and carried it a lot, but that mornin' he'd promised to get a gun fixed for our nephew, and it was easier to carry in his holster. Heseltine wasn't even supposed to be around."

"Heseltine?"

"Bob Heseltine killed him. My brother might have beaten Heseltine, because he was a good man with a gun, but he hadn't a chance. This here gun that I've given you was meant to be used against Heseltine."

I drew the gun again, and looked at it. It was like any other Peacemaker Colt, but—well, it felt different. Maybe it *was* different.

Some guns had a different feel to them, some guns felt right to a man. Usually, it was the getting used to a gun. A man could always shoot a mite better with his own weapon, but this feeling was something different.

"Thanks," I said again, and walked out into the street where the morning sun was bright.

It was warm out there where the sun was shining, but the wind was raw when a man stepped from shelter. The gun rested easy in my holster . . . a gun bought to kill a man. Or rather, for a man to defend himself.

Crossing the street, I picked my way around the mudholes and across the ruts cut deep by freight wagons. Some of them had water standing in them.

Clouds were bunching over the peaks. Some of the peaks you couldn't even see, but the sunshine was still on the street. I turned and looked along it. I would have to be careful now; I could walk nowhere without thinking of who might be waiting for me, or who I might come on unexpectedly.

I had had my first gun battle. I was still alive, and Doc Sites was down.

Nothing in me wanted to kill Kid Reese, or even Heseltine. All I wanted was my money, and then to ride free, to make a place somewhere for myself.

When I was a few steps shy of the Clarendon, a man stepped out from the wall. He was wearing a short sheepskin coat, and his black hat had a torn brim.

"Are you Shell Tucker?" he asked.

"Yes."

He was a stranger, a narrow-faced man with shifty eyes, and I did not like the looks of him very much.

He smiled at me. "Heard about you an' that shootin'. Heard about them fellers makin' off with your money. That there don't seem right."

"It wasn't."

"That Reese now, him an' Heseltine—they've skipped town. They're scared of you."

Maybe I was a kid, but I didn't believe that. Not for a minute. When I remembered the hard, leather-like face of Bob Heseltine and his cold eyes, I felt a chill. He might be many things, but he was not afraid of me.

"I know they've skipped," he said. He glanced up and down the street and stepped a little closer. "I know they've skipped and I know where they are."

72

"You do?"

"They're holed up in a shack the other side of Independence Pass. Sets back in the quakies." I knew that mountain folks often called the aspens "quakies," from their name of quaking aspen. "Good run of water close by," he added. "Figured you'd want to know."

"Thanks."

Con Judy was not in the room when I entered, nor was he in the bar. There was a restlessness in me, and I did not want to wait. They were at the Pass . . . suppose they left there? How long might it be before I found them again?

In our room I quickly wrote a note, then taking up my rifle, my saddlebags and blanket roll, I went down the steps and across the lobby.

My horse was standing three-legged in his stall, and he rolled his eyes at me when I came in, and laid back his ears when I threw the saddle on his back and tightened the cinch. All I was thinking was that they had gone from here, and if I was to have my money back I must follow. Con Judy had his own affairs, and this was mine. Was I a child that I needed him to guide me?

Ducking my head as I rode through the wide door, I turned my horse down the trail. Once I glanced back. A man was standing on the walk staring after me, a man in a short sheepskin coat . . . the man who had told me where I could find Heseltine.

A spatter of rain fell and I slipped into my slicker. It began to rain harder, and the trail became slippery. I rode off it into the sparse grass beside it, and kept on, listening to the sound of rain on my hat and on my shoulders.

The rain would wipe out the tracks, but there were few anyway. The tracks of a lone rider going into Leadville seemed about all.

When I had been riding an hour or more the last shacks had been left behind. On the trail I could see only the lone set of hoofprints going opposite to the way I rode.

It would be dark early, I thought. The water was standing in small pools, and the cold rain slanted across the sky.

I went on. Once my horse slipped on the greasy trail, but he scrambled and got his footing. We kept on for what seemed like a long time, and presently I could see the thin ghost of smoke from a chimney.

The trail took a bend, bringing it nearer the cabin where the smoke lifted. Suddenly I realized I was tired, and that I had been hours in coming this far. Within another hour it would be dark, and here was a chance for a meal, fodder for my horse, and rest.

The rider who had left the tracks I had seen had stopped here, too. In fact, he had mounted his horse by the gate. Despite the rain I could see his tracks clearly in the mud.

The man in the sheepskin coat! The man who had told me where I would find Heseltine. He had stopped here at this house.

He had come into town only minutes, perhaps,

before he talked to me. Why would a man ride in and make such a point of delivering news of where I'd find Heseltine? How would a man from out of town know I was hunting them?

I stared at the house. It was shadowed and still. Only the slow smoke rising, only the tracks of man and horse leading from the stoop. Suddenly I knew this was no place for me.

I had dismounted to open the gate, but suddenly I turned, and catching a closer grip on the reins, I stabbed my toe at the stirrup.

Instantly the evening was ripped apart by the ugly bark of guns. Something hit me and I staggered, half falling against the horse. Something hit me again, but my toe slipped into the stirrup and the forward lunge of the horse sent me into the saddle.

Hanging low in the saddle, I rode on up the trail, away from the house. Behind me another gun slugged the night, and still another. My horse staggered under me, gathered itself, and went on.

Up the hill we went, taking a quick turn into the trees and weaving through them. Behind me I heard a shout, and galloping hoofs.

Through the trees we dodged and turned. The horse was laboring hard now, but it was game. Suddenly I saw a notch in the rocks below me and pulled up, sliding to the ground. As I did so I pulled the draw-string on my blanket roll so that it fell into my hands. Then I grabbed my Winchester and, slapping the horse with the flat of my hand, I turned and slid through the notch. As I went down with a rattle of stones I heard the trotting hoofs of my horse, moving on.

Going through the notch in the rim had landed me on a steep slope of talus. I slid on this broken rock, clinging to rifle and blanket roll, then rolled off it to the grass and went on down a slope through the aspens.

A momentary glimpse down through the trees allowed me to see a canyon wall falling steeply away ahead of me, cloaked with aspen all the way down to the water's edge, at least two hundred yards below.

Hooking an arm around a slender trunk, I held up and listened. Would they come down after me? I doubted it, but I could not be sure. I let myself slide down to a squatting position, concealed by the trunks of the trees and the growth of plants among the aspens.

For a time all I could hear was the slow drop of water from the leaves, and the whispering of the rain as it fell among the trees.

Then I heard, some distance up the slope, a faint movement, and I heard someone call out, "We got him! He's been winged, anyway!"

Suddenly, almost with the shock of a blow, I realized I had been wounded back there. There had been no pain, only the shock of being hit . . . was it once or twice? Then the wild scramble had followed, in which my only thought had been to escape death.

They had suckered me into an ambush. If I had not noticed the tracks at the gate I would have gone on into the cabin and been shot down at point-blank range.

"There's blood here!" came Reese's voice.

"All right." It was Bob Heseltine and his tone was calm. "So we got lead into him. That doesn't mean he's dead."

"You goin' down there after him?" Reese protested.

"We don't need to," Heseltine said. "That's a box canyon, and it opens out right near the cabin. All we have to do is set and wait for him to come out, or die there. There ain't no two ways about it."

They talked some more, but they were closer together by then, and their voices were lower. I could hear nothing more that they said. But I waited.

Slowly my breath came back to me, but with it came a feeling of weakness. I knew I was hit, and was afraid to find out how bad. I didn't want to die, and I was scared, more scared than I'd ever been. It might happen here . . . right here.

I realized there was no reason why I should win and they should not. A bullet had hit me, and a bullet that could hit me could kill me.

Suddenly, crouched under the aspens, I began to shake as if I'd had a chill. Maybe it was because I was scared. Maybe it was just reaction. At the same time I knew that if I could hear them, they could hear me, and I had no idea whether I could move or not.

With infinite care, I eased one knee to the ground and got a tearing spasm of pain in the leg.

It was the leg, then . . . I'd been hit in the leg.

Holding my rifle by the barrel with the butt against the soft ground to steady me, I began to feel with my right hand. I found the wetness of blood, and followed it up my leg. It was right at the top, a raw, bloody place just back of my holster.

Now they were moving off. Their voices dwindled away; their movements faded out. I leaned the rifle against the tree and tugged my left coat sleeve up and the shirt sleeve down. The shirt was new, fresh that morning, a gray flannel one.

Hating to do it, because I'd not had many new shirts in my lifetime, I slipped my knife blade into the flannel and cut loose the cuff and most of the sleeve below the elbow. Then I eased it off and folded it into a thick pad, which I pressed to the wound to stop the bleeding. With part of the string that tied my blanket roll I tied the pad in place.

Then, using the rifle as a crutch, I pushed myself up. My horse was my first concern . . . I would have to have my horse.

Hobbling painfully, then crawling, I made it to the top, but I hadn't gone fifty yards when I saw my horse. It was down, and it was dead.

No horse, and me in a box canyon with no way out. Maybe when they said there was no way, they were thinking of a man on horseback. Most western men thought in terms of using a horse because a man in that country without a horse was usually as good as dead.

Crouching among the aspen, I peered all around. I

could see the rim of the canyon, and it surely looked bad for a man as crippled as I was. Right then I began to take stock.

Nobody knew where I was, so nobody was going to come to help me, even if there'd been anybody to help. Down at the mouth of the canyon were two men who felt it would be better if I was dead—two men and a woman. Only I didn't agree with them, no way at all. I wanted to get out of there, and I wanted a whole skin. And now I was beginning to get mad . . . really mad.

They had stolen our money, they had been responsible for the death of pa, even though those things might be laid at my own door. If I hadn't acted like a fool kid and run off, that horse would never have strayed, and pa might be alive this minute.

All the time I felt aggrieved over them taking our money I couldn't escape the idea that I'd played the fool myself. But they'd tried three times to kill me. Once when they shot into the restaurant, and again when Doc Sites had laid for me in the dark at the foot of the stairs. Now they had tried it a third time, and they might have succeeded. Only now I was mad enough to want to live, mad enough to want to see them in hell, and me with my money back.

I'd lost some blood—they'd seen that. But though they knew I'd been hit, they didn't know how bad. I didn't know how bad myself, but by the size of that wound it didn't look good.

Two things I had to do now. I had to hunt me a hole

and see how bad I was hurt, and then I had to crawl out of that canyon, one way or another. Once out of the canyon I somehow had to get me a horse and get back to Leadville to stay until I was able to ride again.

Pa, he always said there was no stoppin' a man who was set on an idea. He'd told me of men who kept going, even when they was out of their heads, so I told myself what I had to do, and then I set about it.

Just beyond where my horse lay there was an opening in the brush. It might be where a deadfall lay, but it might be a path, and a path would lead to somewhere. Crawling, so's I could drag my leg, I worked my way along the slope, sometimes in and sometimes out of the aspens.

It was a trail, sort of, but it was mighty old. No fresh tracks showed; it hadn't been used in a long time. I turned down the trail, for I needed water, and it was down in the bottom of the canyon.

It began to rain. The grass and lupine around me were already wet, but rain couldn't matter to me now. What I needed was some kind of shelter, some place where I could make a fire, and do something about my wound.

Time to time I thought of that other blow. Had I been shot a second time? No telling . . . but no time to worry about that. The thing to do now was to crawl.

Somewhere along the trail I passed out. Now, in stories I'd read sometimes in those dime-novel books that Reese, Sites, an' me were always swappin' around, when a man passed out he would always come to hisself in a nice bedroom with a pretty girl a-pattin' his brow.

When I come to it was dark, and wet and muddy. I was face down in the trail, and there was no light, not even a star, no fancy bed; and surely no girl a-pattin' me. Only the rain.

"You always thought big about what you'd do when you come to manhood," I said to myself. "Now, boy, you better crawl, or you just ain't a-goin' to make it."

So I crawled.

CHAPTER 7

Lightning flashed and thunder rumbled back in the mountains. I saw the reflection of lightning on the rain-slick rocks. I saw the reflection off the rain-wet grass close to my face. I started to crawl.

I towed behind me my blanket roll with my rifle stuck through the string that tied it. There was sense enough in me to hang onto that.

Once I found a pool on the downhill side of a rock and I dipped my hand into it and drank. I was dry . . . dry inside me anyway—from losin' blood, most likely.

Finally I found a fallen tree, a dead spruce with heavy boughs, and I crawled close to it. It was a fresh fall, the earth likely loosened by the rain. I cut away a few branches with my knife, unrolled my blankets, and crawled in further, muddy and wet though I was.

Twice during the endless night I woke up, once from the pain of my wound, another time from the cold. I felt sick and very tired, and when morning came at last, a gray, dull morning with slanting rain and lowering clouds, my mouth was dry, my head ached, and when I tried to stand I was weak and dizzy. But I knew I must move. If I stayed where I was, in the state I was in, I would surely die.

Staggering, I got to my feet, made a clumsy roll of the blankets, and slipped into my slicker . . . there hadn't been time before. Slinging the blanket roll around my shoulders, I worked my way back up the slope to my horse.

For several minutes I listened to the rain, studied the layout, and when I was sure there was no one about, went up to the saddle.

I got the saddlebags loose, tugged the one from under the horse, and then with them over my shoulder I started up the canyon.

They'd said it was boxed in. Maybe. One thing was sure, the way I felt I wasn't going down canyon to give them a shot at me. As I recalled, there was no cover near the cabin . . . I'd have to break into the open within easy range of it, and they could set right there in the warmth of the cabin and pick me off when I tried to get by.

There was some grub in those saddlebags. Down on the slope I leaned against a tree, because it hurt to bend my leg to sit down, and I ate some jerked beef and a chunk of bread. Then I started on.

My head was throbbing. When I'd made no more than a hundred yards, I had to sit down. I almost fell onto a log and stayed there, panting. My forehead was hot, and my eyes didn't seem to focus right. After a bit I went on, struggling along through trees, over slippery rocks, working my way higher up the canyon.

Presently the canyon narrowed, and a branch came in from the south. Standing there, swaying a little from weakness, I stared up the branch.

You never saw such a mess. There'd been a blow down, leaving hundreds of trees, fallen and dead, crisscrossing the canyon.

Sometimes a howling wind will funnel down such canyons, all its strength channeled into one tremendous blast. Every once in a while in the Rockies you'll come on a canyon like that . . . they seem to suck the winds down them.

This one had blown down most of a small forest, but it had left some trees standing, and others had grown up among them. The place was like a nightmare, but it gave me hope.

Already I could see the rock wall at the branch canyon's end, and it looked sheer and seemed to promise nothing, but I had just an idea that the mess of dead wood might offer something. They had said there was no way out, but I was willing to bet no cowboy had ridden into that canyon, or tried to climb very far through those fallen trees.

Weak as I was, and fuzzy as was my vision as well as my thinking, I had the wild animal's urge to escape, to escape and to hide. At the canyon's entrance I turned and brushed the grass upright where I had stepped. Just the bending over almost caused me to fall, and my hip hurt bad. Turning, I went into the canyon, ducked under one deadfall and half fell over another. I sat down there and swung my legs over a moss-grown boulder and went on. When at last I looked back toward the mouth of the canyon, it could no longer be seen.

Here it was shadowed and still. The whisper of the rain was the only sound, except once in a while the rubbing of one branch against another in some slight stirring of the wind.

Sometimes I fell. My hands were scraped by rough bark when I tried to catch myself. My pack and my rifle caught again and again on branches into which I blundered. But somehow I kept moving because it was in me that I had to move.

I could not let them beat me. I had to get out of here. I had to make them pay for what they had done, but most important, I had to get that money back. I had to get it back for those neighbors of ours in Texas.

Sometimes I passed out and lay still against the wet grass. I wanted to stay and just rest . . . but always I started crawling again. My wound opened and bled, and it hurt, too.

Once when I opened my eyes I found I wasn't among pines any more, but among aspens, so that meant I was getting higher up. Grasping the slender trunk of the nearest tree, I tugged myself up and leaned against it.

The rain had stopped, but there was drifting mist around me. Looking back, I could see nothing of the canyon, for now it was thick with cloud. But on one of the bare, rain-wet peaks above me I could see the reflection of sunlight. Using the trees to help, I pulled myself on, from one to the other.

Aspens are the forest's effort to recover itself, the first trees to spring up after there has been fire, and often they grow on the steep mountainsides below a ridge. They give shelter to wildlife, and to the young evergreens until they are strong enough to stand alone. As the evergreens grow tall, the aspens die out, for they need sunlight and open ground.

This idea worked its way through my fuzzy, wandering thoughts as I struggled along, but a spasm of pain went through me and I fell. I lay gasping, too weak to get up. After a long time I slowly pulled myself up again.

I did not want to go on . . . I wanted to quit. Just to lie down, close my eyes, and not try any more.

That was the way I felt, and that was what I thought I wanted, but something kept urging me on. And suddenly I was at the top. I came out of the trees into a mountain meadow. The far side of the meadow was in sunlight, and when I reached it I stood still, soaking up the warmth.

My eyes had been on it for several minutes before the realization of what I saw reached me.

It was a chimney. A chimney of stone . . . of native stone.

Where there was a chimney there must be a house or cabin. A house or cabin sometimes meant people.

Walking very carefully so that I would not fall, I went through the trees and brush toward the building, which was a cabin. From behind an aspen I studied the layout.

The cabin was small. There was no sign of life any-where around, but there were some horse droppings in the yard that might not be old. With the recent rain it was hard to tell. There was a corral and an open-faced shed.

Walking slowly, my rifle ready in my hands, I went around to the front. No tracks since the rain. A path led away from the cabin and down into the trees.

The door opened easily under my hand. Inside, the cabin was spotless. There was a neatly made bed, a fireplace with the fire laid, and a floor that had been scrubbed . . . something unusual in the mountains.

A blanket hung over a door to a room beyond. Pushing it aside, I saw another bedroom, this one with curtains. In a crudely made wardrobe were some women's fixings.

I put my gun down and laid my blanket roll on a bench, and then I lit the fire and put on a kettle. I knew that I was working against time. That I was in bad shape, nobody needed to tell me, and it was time I bathed the wound in my hip and discovered what else had happened to me.

Weak as I was, I had no idea whether I'd get through the day or not. Taking off my slicker, I unslung my gun-belt, blinking my eyes in dull amazement at what I saw.

The bullet had evidently hit my belt, exploding at least two cartridges and leaving that part of my belt mostly blown away. The explosion had torn that hole in my side. Suddenly scared, I peeled down my pants and lifted my shirttail free.

The folded flannel had stopped the blood, but where it didn't cover the wound I could see the shine of a fragment of metal from the exploded shell. If that stuff was all through the wound I was in mighty serious trouble.

I hunted around for coffee, but didn't find any. There was some tea, and I put some in a pot and poured boiling water over it.

Then with a white cloth I found in the room I began to soak the edges of the wound and to sponge it off carefully. Twice the cloth caught on bits of metal, and each time I got them out with care. The wound had begun to fester a little, so they came free easy.

Finally I could lift the flannel pad out, and with hot water I cleaned out the wound. It was tough working on it, for I had to twist around to get at it. I found several pieces of cartridge casing and hoped I was getting them all. A couple of times I stopped to gulp down hot tea. The room was warm and I felt dizzy, but I knew I had to get done what I'd started.

A time or two I got up and hobbled around, trying to

find something to use on the wound. There was half a bottle of whiskey, but I hesitated to use that, although I had taken a stiff jolt of it myself. It seemed a shameful waste of good whiskey to flush out the wound with it, but that was what had been done many's the time on the Plains, I knew. I was fixing to use it when I found some turpentine.

Mixing some of that with hot water, I bathed the wound out, and if I was sweating before I surely was then. I made another pad from some of the clean white cloth I'd found and put it into the wound and tied it there.

I gulped down more tea, and then, putting my rifle alongside the bed and my pistol handy, I just lay down and passed out.

The last thing I remembered was worrying about my muddy boots. I'd not had a moment to get them off, and I feared to struggle with them, for it might start the bleeding again.

Those muddy boots, and the firelight flickering on the walls . . . It seemed to me it was raining again, too.

CHAPTER 8

The cold awakened me. I lay shivering, uncovered, on the bed. The cabin was dark; rain fell on the roof. The fire was out. Lightning flashed, momentarily lighting the room. Alone in a strange place, I knew I was sick . . . sicker than I'd ever been.

Rolling over on the bed, I swung my muddy boots to the floor. My head was burning with fever, my mind searching through a fog of pain for the right thing to do. Stumbling to the fireplace, I fumbled with a poker and stirred a few dying coals among the gray ashes and the charred ends of sticks.

With an effort, I clustered some of them near the coals and blew on them. Smoke rose, but there was no flame. I looked around for something for kindling, and finally tore a few handfuls of straw from the broom.

A little tongue of fire fed on the straw, and made a quick, bright blaze, and I put on pieces of bark and slender sticks to keep it burning. I nudged the pot, and saw that steam still rose from it. Again I drank tea, sipping it slowly.

Huddling near the fire, I shivered. One side of me was icy cold, the other burning. I fed more sticks into the fire, then wrestled a heavier piece and still another into the blaze.

Then for the first time I saw a bootjack, and hooking my boot into it, I managed to draw off one and then the other. After that I tumbled back to the bed and crawled under the covers. At first I still shivered, but at last I grew warm and slept again.

It was a restless sleep, with shifting scenes. In one I stood alone in an icy field and saw a line of men on horseback charging down upon me. Their knees were drawn up like jockeys', and they wore black leather shields and carried curved swords. I fought and struggled as one rushed at me, swinging a blade. I felt it bite deep, and I fell.

For a long time I lay there in the cold, and then my eyes opened.

I had fallen to the floor; the fire was down again, and the room was still dark. Crawling to the fireplace, I fed sticks into the coals and the flames leaped up. I listened to the wind and rain . . . how long would this night last? The wind lashed the trees outside, and rain whipped against the cabin. I managed to pull myself to the window, but I could see nothing, only the blackness and the windowpane running with water. Somehow I got back onto the bed, and could only stare up at the ceiling.

Later, I once more got up and added fuel to the fire. The supply of wood was getting low. Soon it would be gone.

Again I slept, and again there was nightmare. Only this time I was on a great slippery rock with waves breaking over it, cold waves that rushed over me as I clung to the rock.

I dug my fingers into a crack, and with each wave that came I was stiff with fear. My fingers became numb. How long could I hold on? . . .

And then I was awake and it was day. The rain had stopped and the wind was gone. The cabin still stood. I was too weak to move. My wound had bled some more, but that had stopped. My mouth was dry, but I had no wish to stir. My fingers did move, to feel for the gun . . . it was still there.

For a long time I dozed. But at last I was awake, really awake. Light from the windows was the dull light of a cloudy day, or maybe the light of evening.

Turning my head, I could see the fireplace. Some coals still remained, and a thin thread of steam rose from the pot. Only two sticks were left.

When I tried to rise my head swam, but I made it. Without fire, I doubted if I could survive another night. I got up slowly, added the two sticks to the fire, and poured another cup of tea.

Huddling there, I drank it. Then with an effort I got to the bed, took up the gun, thrust it into my waistband, and stumbled to the door.

For a moment I leaned against the doorjamb, watching outside. Not thirty feet from the door there was a wood-pile. Holding my hand against my side, I made it to the pile and gathered three or four sticks together, about all I figured I could carry. I was just stooping to pick them up when I heard hoofbeats on the trail . . . more than one horse.

Clumsily, because of my side, I dropped to one knee. The woodpile was about five feet high, and thick through. Wood had been taken from the place where I crouched, leaving a notch in the pile, and in this I waited, gun in hand. Four-foot lengths of wood almost surrounded me.

Heseltine's voice was the first I heard. "Aw, he's dead, Kid! We're wastin' time."

"I'll believe it when I see it. We figured to have him twice before."

"There's no way out of that canyon, and even if there was, how could he crawl all the way over that mountain? Anyway, the canyon heads up off south of here."

"Just the same, I'm lookin' around."

A saddle creaked, and footsteps sloshed over the wet earth. I heard a step on the porch; momentary silence, then the door creaked open.

"Nobody in there," Reese said doubtfully. "The fire's almost out."

"If you two will stop being such fools," a girl's voice said, "we can be on our way before somebody comes back and wants to know what we're doin' here."

"So?"

"What are you going to tell them, Kid?" Ruby Shaw's tone was contemptuous. "Everybody in Leadville knows we've had trouble, so if Tucker shows up dead, they'll know we were hunting him."

"She's right, Kid."

Reese still hesitated, but finally, grumbling, he went to his horse. Stirrup leather creaked again, and for a moment I had a wild urge to step out just as they rode away. I was sure to get one of them . . . maybe both.

Good sense warned me. In my condition I couldn't even be sure of putting a bullet close to them . . . even be sure of holding a gun at arm's length.

Dry-mouthed, gun in hand, I listened to them ride away. Slowly I holstered my gun and picked up the armful of wood. I'd taken two staggering steps toward the house when a voice said, behind me, "Thought there for a minute I was goin' to see a shootin'."

I stood very still.

Walk on, I told myself, walk right up to the steps. If he was going to shoot he would have done it already. Walk right inside and put the wood down. Get your hands empty.

Don't look around, don't turn, just act as if you didn't even hear.

I started toward the cabin. At the steps I paused automatically to scrape the mud from my boots on the scraper there, but I did not look around. I went on inside and carefully dropped the wood into the woodbox.

Behind me, in the doorway, a dry voice said, "Mister, I'm friendly, so when you turn around your hands better be empty."

Slowly, I turned.

A wiry man was standing in the doorway. He held a rifle in his hands and it covered me. Had I planned to draw, I would never have gotten halfway around before he'd nailed me.

Then I saw something else. From a window which had been soundlessly pushed open another rifle was pointed at me.

"I never drew against a full house," I said. "Come in and make yourselves to home."

The man stepped inside. He was all of fifty, maybe older, and he had a lean old face that looked hard enough to have worn out two or three bodies.

"Come in, Vash. This is him I was tellin' you of."

A girl appeared behind him, carrying a rifle. She was young, slender, and large-eyed.

With her free hand she brushed a strand of hair back from her eyes and came on into the room, seeming to take very short steps. Without thinking, my eyes dropped to her feet. She wore men's shoes.

When I looked up, she was walking by me, her face flushed.

The man pushed the door shut behind her, then glanced around the room. "You et?"

"No, sir."

He looked at me and said, "You'd better set down, son. You look as if you're all in."

"I've been shot," I said, and dropped weakly onto the bed. "They got lead into me. I done the best I could with it."

"We'll eat," the old man replied, "then Vash will see to it. She's good with gunshot wounds. Started learnin' on me when she was ten year old."

She had taken off her man's coat. She had a figure, all right, and maybe wasn't as young as she looked there to start. She might be all of sixteen.

She picked up the teapot, looked into it. "Well, you had sense enough for that, anyway."

She went about fixing something to eat whilst the old man barred the door and put up the shutters. "Seen you down to town," he commented. "You've stirred up some talk."

He hung up his hat and coat, added wood to the fire,

then sat down and took a pipe from his pocket. He held it up. "Learned it from the Injuns, as a boy. Been at it ever since." He gestured toward the girl. "Her ma was an Ogalalla."

"I hear they were the best of the Sioux," I said, "and had the handsomest women."

"Well, depends where a body stands, I reckon. If'n they had good chiefs they reckoned to be right pleasant folk often enough. Them Hunkpappas now, I had trouble with them a time or two, and with the Arickaras.

"I come west in '33. Trapped fur up north, lived with the Sioux for nigh onto twenty year."

He struck a match. He jerked his head in the direction the riders had gone. "Them the ones you're after?" I nodded.

"You had you a chance."

"I decided against it. Didn't know whether I was strong enough to draw a bead on them. I might have taken one, but the other one would have killed me, weak as I am. I let 'em ride off. There'll be another day."

"Well," the old man said dryly, "you ain't a total damn fool."

He paused for a minute. "When you tangle with them, boy, don't let that woman go without judgin' her careful. She's worse'n either of them, I'm thinking."

"Her?"

"Yes, her. She's poison mean, and quick with a gun,

too. She killed a man up to Weaverville, a year or so back."

As I sat on the bed the warmth of the fire after the cold outside was making me sleepy. I tried to hold my eyes open, and for a while there I could manage it. Then somewhere along the line I just faded out.

When my eyes opened again the room was dark except for the firelight. I stayed still, wondering what had happened.

My boots had been taken off, and my pants. For a time I just stared up at the ceiling. Then I swung my feet to the floor, and that girl was sitting by the fire, looking into the coals.

She turned her head when I sat up, and she said, "Well, you took long enough! You'd better have some of this soup now."

"Thanks."

I was almighty weak, but I made it to the fireside and sat down on the wide hearth. The cabin was warm now, and I could hear the easy snores of the old man.

"You been living here long?" I asked.

"Well, pa built this place, maybe fifteen years ago when he was down this way. We've come to it two or three times."

"Prospector?"

"Hunter, mostly. Oh, he looks around. He finds rock now and again, but he would rather shoot meat and sell it to the miners. Pa likes to come here. He reads a lot."

"Him?"

She looked up quickly. "Don't you be underrating pa. He had ten years of schooling before he came west, and he went to good schools. His name is Lander Owen, and he comes of an educated family, only he liked it in the West. You should have heard Mr. Denig and pa talking . . . and Mr. Denig was one of the smartest men there was."

"Never heard of him."

"We can't all be smart. He was a fur trader, came west the same year pa did, I reckon, and he married an Indian girl . . . two of them, in fact."

"That makes it nice."

She gave me a quick, angry look. "His first wife wasn't well. Should he throw her out because of that? A man has to have a wife . . . so Mr. Denig just taken on another one.

"He knew more about Indians than almost any white man I ever knew. He wrote about them. Some of his things were published back east. Folks came west to talk to him about Indian ways. Edwin Thompson Denig was his name."

She was proud, and I liked the way she was quick to speak, chin up, eyes flashing.

Denig. I made a note of the name—I surely had a lot to learn.

The soup was hot, all right, and it tasted good. I finished the bowl and had another, and then sleep began to catch up with me. I dearly wished to talk. It was the first time I'd talked to a girl—a young one—in months.

"Your pa called you Vash. Is that your name?"

"Vashti. Pa got it from the Bible, but it's a Persian name. A man told pa it meant beautiful one."

"He sure named you right. You are beautiful."

She flushed, shot me a quick glance, and then looked away. "You're just saying that because you want more soup. Well, I'll give you some—you don't have to say it."

"I meant it. And I can't eat any more soup."

"You don't like my soup?"

"Sure, I like it. Here, give me another bowl."

I surely didn't need that last bowl. I was already about as full up as a man could get, but I didn't want her to think I was slighting her cooking, so I ate it, down to the last drop.

Her grandpa's name was The Swan, she told me, and he'd been a great chief and a fine orator. Well, I'd heard talk of him. In Dodge, where we sold our cattle, there was talk about him from an old buffalo hunter we met. He'd told us that while The Swan had been chief of the Ogalallas they had been better fed, better clothed, and in less trouble than any time.

While she was washing the soup bowl I went to the bed and was asleep almost as soon as I stretched out. And there was no nightmare this time.

CHAPTER 9

It was light when I woke up, and the old man was gone from the cabin. Vashti was working around, but when she saw that I was awake she came over and looked at me critically.

"You should shave more often."

Now that was a contrary sort of attitude. "Ma'am," I said, "I been busy saving my hide. I had no time to think of it."

"You've time now. I'll heat some water."

Meanwhile she put some bacon in the pan, and I could smell it, and was getting hungrier and hungrier. After a while I sat up and pulled on my pants when her back was turned, not fastening my belt tight because I wanted no pressure on that wound.

"You showed sense getting that metal out of there," she said. "At least you didn't forget everything."

When I started to speak, she cut me off. "Pa brought your saddle down. Got it off your horse."

"He went through all that brush? And those deadfalls?"

"There's an easier way, but it's roundabout. Pa knows every trail in these mountains, I do believe."

She brought me some hot water, soap, and a razor, and I shaved. And it felt good.

By the time I'd finished she had put food on the table. She poured coffee and sat down across the table from me.

"Well," she said at last, "you're not a bad-looking boy when you're shaved."

"I'm no boy."

She let that pass, but said, "What do you plan to do now?"

"Follow them. Soon as I'm able."

"I would think you'd had enough of that. Next time they'll surely kill you."

"No, ma'am, they won't. They suckered me into a trap."

"Twice," she said dryly. "You played the fool twice. Why walk into a dark hall when you know men are waiting for you? Or go riding off because some passerby tells you where to find them? If I were Bob Heseltine I'd not be worried."

Well, sir, she was getting under my skin. My face was flushing, but I held my tongue.

"At least it didn't hurt your appetite any," she said, as I finished the bacon. "Will you have some more coffee?"

"Please."

"Well," she said, "somebody taught you manners, anyway. Was it Mr. Judy?"

"What do you know about him?"

"He's your friend, isn't he? Pa says you've been getting about with all those high-toned, high-falutin' folks down to Leadville. Pa thinks quite a lot of Mr. Judy."

"Seems as if ever'body does. I wonder how a man gets to be liked that much?"

"There's nothing so surprising in that, Shell Tucker. A man is liked because he is likable, and most often I suspect because he likes other people. I've heard pa talk about Con Judy.

"He's had a lot of men from time to time on mining and railroad jobs, and he's always been honest with them. He wants a day's work for a day's pay, but he stands by those who work for him, as well as those he works for, and if anybody has any argument Con is ready to meet them anyway they choose—only most of them don't choose."

"He's a good friend," I said. "I can say that."

I was feeling weaker than a cat. It was good just to sit still and enjoy the sunlight of the day. And a comforting thing it was to have Vashti moving around, doing little things to straighten up the place. Pa and me had been batching these last years, and it was surprising, watching her, to see how much we'd overlooked doing in keeping a place looking shipshape. Vashti, she never missed a thing, and no wasted motion, either.

"Is that all you have to do? Sit and watch me?"

"I was admiring how handy you were. I never did see a girl do so much with so few moves."

We talked a bit, and then I stretched out so's I could rest. I thought about Heseltine and Reese. More than likely they were gone, but they might come back. I'd have to be ready for that.

After a while I sat up and found the stuff Owen used in cleaning his rifle, and I cleaned mine, and my six-shooter, too. Vashti looked at me from time to time, but she said nothing.

Meanwhile I was studying about those two men. All I'd figured about Ruby Shaw would still hold true, I thought. She wouldn't want to be holed up in some cabin with two irritable outlaws, even if she was the girl of one of them. She'd want a town where money could be spent, where she could have some fancy clothes and wear them, and so far all she'd had was trouble. Come to think of it, she wouldn't be thinking very kindly of me.

"I should think you'd want to get a job and make something of yourself," Vashti said suddenly.

Took me a moment to get my thoughts in line. "I've got to get those men to give me back that money," I said. "I swore I'd pay back every dime we were trusted with. I've got it to do."

"Maybe you could earn it faster."

"It would take me years, ma'am. Years, to make that much. And those men have got to be made to pay for what they've done."

We talked the question back and forth, but in the midst of it I fell asleep again. Which was probably the smartest thing I could have done.

When I woke up, who should be sitting by the fire but Con Judy. "When you get shot up," he said as I opened my eyes, "you take care to do it where you have a pretty nurse right close at hand."

Vashti blushed, but she was pleased, too. Especially as it was coming from Con, who had a way with him.

"It's the only way to go," I said, grinning at him. "How'd you get up here?"

"Lander sent word. He figured I'd be worried, and I was, you taking off like that." Then he added, "They're gone. They pulled their freight, all three of them."

"You went over there?"

"Thought I might have a word with them. That was before I ran into Lander Owen—Lander and I have been friends for some time. But I'd already started tracing you down. I got a tip in Leadville that Heseltine had been making inquiries about that cabin, so I went up there."

"They might have killed you."

"Might have. But I might have done some shooting, too. Anyway, Heseltine would think twice before taking a shot at me. If he did that he wouldn't be safe anywhere in Colorado."

He paused and refilled his cup; then he asked, "What are your plans?"

"To get well, and get on their trail. I'm going to track them down no matter how long it takes." I hadn't really thought of it that way, but suddenly I knew that what I said was true.

They had robbed a boy and a wounded man. The wounded man was dead, but somewhere along the line something had happened to that boy. They had tried to kill me, and I had put one of them down with lead, but they had almost gotten me this time. Next time I would be shooting first.

Something else had happened, too. The cold eyes of Bob Heseltine no longer worried me. I'd been pushed around and shot at, but I was no longer afraid. Wary, yes, but not afraid, as I admitted to myself I had been.

"A man does what he has to do," Lander said quietly.

"You lived with Indians too long, Lander," Con said. "I'd like Tucker to drop the whole thing. I've some contracts and I need a good young man to help me." He looked over at me. "You could make a good bit more than working for wages. I need a man to help me ramrod a track-laying job."

"All right," I said. "I'll help, and when the job is finished, I'll go after them. It might be a good thing to let them relax a little."

"It will be thirty days before we can get started," Con said. "Lander will be working with me, too."

Thirty days? I'd be well long before then, and could do a little scouting.

The days passed slowly, but pleasantly enough. Daytimes I'd talk with Vashti, and I'd help her get fuel in for the fire, breaking branches for kindling, as I couldn't take a chance on swinging an axe, for fear it would open my wound.

It wasn't until I began moving around that I found where that other bullet had struck.

My gun belt was a kind of fancy one, with loops for cartridges and silver plaques separating one set of twelve from another. One of those bullets had hit one of those silver plates, glanced off, and gone about its business, but the wallop it gave me left a big bruise on my back and side. The second bullet must have hit me as I was turning from the first shot.

When I could get outside to sit in the sun I saw what a grand place they'd picked for that cabin.

It was on a small knoll. Down in the trees there was a corral with several horses, and a long slope covered with aspens. The cabin stood in a grove of their slim pale trunks, and I loved the whispering of their leaves.

There were squirrels around, and birds, and it was almighty pleasant just sitting in the sun and watching things. Sometimes I'd walk out from the house and sit down on a stump left from the time they cut logs for the cabin. The squirrels would pay me no mind, just chasing one another through the trees and along the ground.

There's a good deal of life goes on in an aspen grove. Elk and beaver love the bitter inner bark, squirrels and chipmunks come looking for the berries and seeds among the brush that often grows along the ground; Rocky Mountain nuthatches, blue jays, and woodpeckers are always there, as well as a dozen other kinds of birds and animals. Harebells, bluebells, cowslips, and pink roses often cover the ground.

When I was looking and listening in the stillness like that it seemed I could almost feel the mountains changing, for no matter how changeless and timeless they may seem, they are never twice the same.

Lander Owen came up from where he'd been chopping wood. He squatted on his heels alongside the porch and nodded toward the mountains. "A man can always learn from them," he said. "The Indians know a lot no white man will ever know, and they don't tell what they know. They expect you to know it, too, and they don't feel they have to tell what they know, the way a white man does.

"Maybe if they'd had a written language it would have been different, for the Indian has a great feeling for words, and the sounds of words. Surely there would have been poets among them, as there were artists."

"I never knew much about them except that they like to fight."

"They are a warlike people, generally speaking. Now and again some chief would see the wisdom of avoiding trouble, and his people would usually profit by it.

"Vashti's grandfather, Ma-ga-ska, The Swan, was a great warrior, but he was a shrewd ruler and a man of great natural ability. Denig used to say that his people were the most trustworthy of any Indians he knew, but they had been at war with the Crows as far back as anybody could remember. But as long as The Swan was alive they had no trouble with the white man."

Lander Owen was silent then for a while, but presently he said, "Son, you should have seen this country when I first came into it. There were mighty few white men, and not so many Indians as you'd think, and a man could ride for days and see nobody at all. He could drink from any stream and find food in most places, and there were millions of wild horses running free on the Plains. Now men are coming into the country and soon you'll see cities growing up."

"Cities? Out here?"

"Boy, a beaver builds dams because it's his nature, and a man builds cities for the same reason, I suppose. It's likely men can't help themselves any more than a beaver can . . . or the ant that builds an anthill, or the bees a hive.

"There are men who seem to have a compulsion to build—to build buildings, railroads, or bridges; to sink mines, to build fortunes. It's man's nature. Some make it through luck, but the ones who last are those who put one foot ahead of the other, one stone on another. If you build to last, you've got to build with work and with patience."

What was I going to build, I wondered. Anything at all? Or was I just going to find those two men and make them give up what was left of our money. I didn't like to think of what I wasn't doing, so I shook it off. I'd heard old men talk before, like pa.

But when I thought of him I remembered how right he had been about Reese and Sites, and how wrong I'd been. Well, that was one time. Now I knew better, and I was going to find those men. And I had several weeks before Con Judy got started with his kind of building.

Lander Owen went off now about his business and

I still sat there in the sun, riding my mind down the possible trails those two might have gone. I wasn't going to let up on them until I had them by the short hair.

It would have been easier, in some ways, if I'd never met Con Judy. He was my friend, maybe the first real friend I ever had, but he had opened doors for me that maybe he'd better left closed. He had introduced me to men who were doing something in the world, men who had the respect of their communities. All of them were building things to last; and me, I was just hunting two men who had taken our money and tried to kill me.

Five days later, on a horse I bought from Lander Owen, I took the trail.

I didn't aim to ride into Leadville, because I didn't want Con Judy to talk me out of it, or anybody else. I was giving myself three weeks to find them, and if by that time I hadn't, I would double back, take Con's job, and stay on it until I earned some money.

Vashti was there to say good-bye, although she didn't hold with my going. She said it, and then turned her back on me and walked away. I was looking after her, thinking I should say something I hadn't said, when Lander stepped up close.

"Boy, Con is probably right, and Vash, too. Me, I lived with redskins too long. I figure you got it to do, so I'll tell you this: When they pulled out they were headed for the Frying Pan country, and they'd teamed up with two more outlaws, Burns King and Pit Burnett."

Burnett I'd seen a couple of times in Leadville. He had been a hanger-on around State Street, and had been pointed out as a gunman, a mine guard, and a trouble-hunter. King I knew nothing about, and said so.

"Well," Lander Owen said dryly, "when he was hangin' around Prescott there were a lot of holdups in Black Canyon. He drifted up Nevada way and there were a couple up there. I don't know anything, but it seems to me . . ."

It seemed to me, too. Heseltine was not teaming up with any other outlaws because he wanted company, but because he had something in mind.

And what about the money? Was that all gone? I felt my stomach kind of turn over at the thought.

Now I knew what I was going to do. I was going to ride up Frying Pan way, and then I was going to cross over and find out the nearest stage route. And I was going to get me a job riding shotgun. If they wanted to hold up a stage, I would be there waiting for them.

I'd ride shotgun for free, if it had to be. When they came hunting I'd be sitting right up on top, ready for them.

CHAPTER 10

The man at the stage station was named Rollins. He looked up at me from under a green eyeshade, then sat back in his swivel chair. He was a man of forty-odd, already a little gray around the temples, but he had a capable way about him.

His eyes were blue and steady, and he studied me a moment before he answered me. "You want to ride shotgun? What makes you think we need a shotgun guard?"

"Bob Heseltine and Kid Reese are headed this way. They've got Pit Burnett and Burns King with them."

"Oh? Heseltine, is it? You wouldn't be Shell Tucker, would you?"

"I would." I was surprised. "How did you know that?"

"There's been talk." He leaned forward in his chair and shuffled the papers in front of him. He seemed to be considering my application for the job. "You realize, of course, that the shotgun guard will be the one they're looking for first? They'd blast you off the top before you could lift a finger."

"I've thought about that. I had an idea I'd ride inside. You say you haven't had a guard, so it's likely they won't be expecting one."

Rollins settled back again. "All right. What do you want to do?"

"Have the job, stay out of sight, and make one run over the route to sort of get the lay of the land. I'd like to talk to your drivers, too."

Rollins shook his head. "No, that's too risky. One of them might say something. I'll tell you what I'll do. We have a bed in the back of the station here. We can fix you up there, you can eat and sleep there, and you can talk to Tobin Dixie. He's our smartest driver, and very likely he's the one you'll have. He knows every inch of the route, knows it the way you know the shape of your face."

That night, sitting on the edge of a cot in the back room at the stage station, I listened to Dixie. He was a small, wiry man with sandy hair, lean jaws constantly busy with Navy plug, and shrewd, careful eyes. Right off, I liked him. There was something about him that told you he'd stand with you.

"It ain't so easy, Tucker. The first ten mile is open country, right out in the sagebrush. There's no cover, none a-tall, and no place to hide a horse . . . not even room to hide your hat.

"Then the road goes uphill for three, four mile. Winding road, lots of cover. There's one big gray boulder that's been used by half a dozen holdup men. Sticks right out into the road.

"After that it's all downhill, right to the next station. There's lots of brush and boulders, but the stage is moving too fast to stop it easy. Only one holdup man tried that stretch, and the stage just ran off and left him standing there."

We talked quite a spell, and when Tobin Dixie had gone I stretched out on the bed, put my hands behind my head and began to study on what I'd heard.

A logical place would be on the slow upgrade, but that didn't seem what Heseltine would do. Maybe on top? I thought about that, but didn't like it either.

The thing was, I was going to have to guess right. If I didn't, I could get myself shot . . . and probably would anyway.

On the downhill side the stage would be rolling too fast . . . but suppose, for some reason, it wasn't? Suppose for some reason it had to go slow?

The more I studied on it the more likely it seemed, if it could be worked. But how could a man slow down a stage without being on it? If one of them did ride the stage they would see me, and I would see them before they ever left town. It didn't seem a very sure possibility.

A boulder or a log in the road? No, the driver would know right away something was wrong, and would either turn around, if there was room, or go around the obstacle, or get shaped up to fight.

Bob Heseltine was no fool, and he wouldn't choose a place where they were likely to be ready for him. All the way up that slow, winding hill they would be set for trouble, and when they slowed at the top to take a breather, they would be sitting with their guns ready. On the long ride downhill they would be relaxed, feeling the danger was over. The question was, how could the stage be slowed down without its being a warning.

Tobin Dixie had gone over the road for me thoroughly, but there's nothing like seeing a trail for yourself. So I had that to do, if I could do it without being seen.

At the same time, holed up as I was, I had a chance to study the situation. I did not want to kill anybody, and particularly I didn't want to kill either Reese or Heseltine. I wanted my money back, and I was sure they hadn't spent all the money as yet . . . they hadn't had time.

It seemed likely they had some idea in mind that called for more money than they had. Instead of just whooping it up in saloons, they must have an idea of going somewhere else and starting something else that required more money; or maybe they wanted to go to the elegant hotels back east or on the coast and really live it up. I decided Ruby Shaw might be wanting just that, and from all I'd heard Ruby was a girl who got what she wanted . . . up to a point.

There was no other reason that I could see for them to start on the outlaw trail again so soon. Not with money in their pockets that the law couldn't touch them for.

One of them would come to town to scout around, and no doubt they also had somebody in town already who knew when the stage would be carrying money. Did that somebody know about me? I had to chance it that he didn't, and make sure he didn't learn anything about me. Which meant I had to stay holed up.

There was a peekhole in the wall where a man could see what went on in the office, and there was a window that looked out on the street. The building next door cut off the view, but sitting by that window a man could watch folks pass for a few yards on this side of the street, and several times that distance across the way.

About noon on the second day a man walked up the street and leaned against the awning pole and began to build a cigarette. He was a lean, swarthy man I had not seen before. He looked like any cowpoke, except that his boots were polished, he wore fancy Mexican spurs, and his outfit looked a mite better than most cowhands could afford.

When he cupped his hands to light his smoke, his eyes came over to the stage station, held there for a moment, then drifted along. He stalled around there until he had smoked three cigarettes, then he walked off down the street, but later he came back and stood against the front of a building just within range of my view.

There was a bench there, and after a while he sat down on it and spent a good part of the afternoon right there. And while he studied the station and watched what went on, I studied him.

He carried a six-shooter in a holster on his right hip, but he also wore a coat, whereas most riders simply wore a vest, because it gave them shoulder room and had pockets for tobacco, matches, and such-like.

As I watched, he put a hand into the left side of his coat several times—a movement I was sure he wasn't aware of. What was there that occupied his mind? Money? Could be. A weapon? More likely. There was no bulge that I could see at this distance, but why not a derringer—insurance against those little occurrences that sometimes happen?

It would be a thing to remember.

The next day the man with the polished boots was no longer around, but there was another one, and this one I had no trouble recognizing, for it was Reese.

He was less patient than the first man, who I surmised was Pit Burnett. Reese would sit for a short while, then move off and stroll along the street, and presently return. Everybody on the street was too busy to pay them much mind, for western towns had few men just idling time away. Every man had a job to do and he was busy doing it.

The next day I was supposed to take my trip on the stage to study the route, and I was restless to be going. But as I waited there in the back room, all of a sudden a buckboard came rolling up the street with two men on the driver's seat, one of them carrying a Winchester. Riding behind was another man, also armed. Reese was half asleep on the bench across the way, but when that buckboard showed up he got up as quick as if he'd been bee-stung. On the side of it was painted the words, GOLD HILL MINING CO.

When I looked at the bench again Reese was gone.

This then was it. I wasn't going to get a chance to

take that first ride over the road. This shipment would be going out on tomorrow's stage, and I'd be riding with it.

After a few minutes the buckboard rolled away and I got up. One of the men who had come with it had evidently remained behind.

Rollins opened the door and stuck his head into the room. "Come in here, Shell. I want you to meet somebody."

He was a short man, square and heavy around the middle, but the eyes that measured me as I went into the room were sharp and steady.

"Shell, meet Do Silva. He'll be riding with you."

"We can use him," I said, but I was not happy over it, and he noticed it.

He looked at me thoughtfully. "You do not like me, *amigo?*"

"I've got nothing against you," I told him. "You look like quite a man. Only I was on this deal alone and was planning to handle it alone."

He shrugged. "I can listen."

I hesitated. "Well, I don't know how I can handle it, only I don't want to kill Kid Reese or Bob Heseltine unless I have to."

He just looked at me, so I explained. "All right, unless we have to. Who are the others?"

When I told him about Burns King and Pit Burnett, he shrugged again. "They are bad men, *amigo.* Burnett will shoot. So will King if he is pushed. I do not know the others."

"You saw Reese. He was the puncher who got up off the bench as your buckboard rolled by. I saw you look at him."

"That was Reese? He was watching?"

"Uh-huh. And before him Burnett was here. At least, I think it was Burnett." I described him, and the Mexican nodded.

"I think so. I think it is him."

The more I talked to Silva, the better I liked him. He was thirty-five or so, not over five feet five, but he must have weighed close to two hundred pounds. Only a little of it was fat. He moved quickly and easily, and I figured he would handle himself well in a battle.

We sat and talked, drank coffee and ate frijoles, tortillas, and beef, and speculated on tomorrow. I explained to him my thinking about the country—the slow climb, the hilltop, and then the fast downhill trip. He listened but offered no comment, and I had no idea whether he agreed or not.

When morning came it was cloudy and cool, with a feel of rain in the air. Nobody was around when we put the solidly built chest that held the gold into the boot under the driver's feet. Tobin Dixie was driving, Do—it was short for Fernando, I learned—would ride on the box. I would ride inside. There were no passengers.

"Are there any stops?" I asked. "I mean where we might pick up passengers?"

"Two," Tobin answered, "but we don't often pick up

anybody until along toward the end of the week. Friday, maybe."

There were few people on the street when we rolled out. Tobin Dixie was on the box, and he started at a good clip. Seated in the stage, I leaned back and got set to get a little rest while we crossed the flats, before we came to the hills.

When the stage started the long climb, I sat up and kept my eyes open. There was no sign of movement anywhere except a bunch of antelope that took off as we approached, and a couple of jackrabbits. With a pair of field glasses belonging to Rollins, I checked out the country. Once I thought I saw dust, but it vanished and there was nothing more.

We made the climb and drew up for a breather. Silva got down from the box and walked back.

"How are they going to stop us?" he asked. "Do you think they'd shoot the horses?"

"I doubt it." I was puzzled. All the signs had pointed to a holdup. We had the gold aboard and the bandits knew it. They also knew Silva was riding shotgun, and that he was a dangerous man, but an express messenger is wide open to being killed from ambush. Almost nobody ever shot a stage driver . . . that was almost as bad as killing a woman or a child. In the minds of most western men a stage driver was something special, and outlaws had long made it a practice to leave them alone . . . not that there hadn't been accidents.

We had stopped on the crest, a bank of earth and

rock about six feet high on our right, the slope falling steeply away on our left. The slope was dotted with stunted pines. A few rocks had fallen off the bank and lay across the road. A camp-robber jay came down and perched on one of the rocks near the top of the bank.

"Tobin," I asked suddenly, "are there any banks down there along the road? Any cuts the road goes through?"

"Sure. There's a dozen, anyway. This here road was cut and blasted out of the mountainside."

"Ever have any rockfalls along the road?"

"Ever' time there's a storm." He glanced at me, his expression suddenly thoughtful. "Why?"

"What do you do when you see a rock fall?"

"Why, slow up, of course. Some of those rocks are big enough to upset a stage, and a man has to be careful of his horses."

Silva had turned around and was looking at me. "You're right. That could be it."

Tobin turned around. "Let's go see," he said.

"The second or third fall, probably. I doubt if it would be the first one." As I spoke, he nodded, then swung up to the box.

Opening the shotgun, I checked it. Two cartridges. There was a box on the seat beside me and I dropped half a dozen from it into my pocket, then took the thong off the hammer of my six-shooter.

The stage started to move before Silva was quite seated. Tobin jumped the horses into a run and started down the grade. He put the horses around bends as if no such things were there, making time while he could.

We had run for nearly a mile before I suddenly heard a yell from Tobin and the stage began to slow down. From the side window I could see a spill of rocks and small boulders across the road.

We slowed up and drove around them, and just as Tobin was about to let the horses go again there was a yell from the bank above the stage.

"Hold up there! Move those horses and I'll kill you!"

The voice, I was sure, was Heseltine's. At the same moment three men dropped into the road and ran toward the stage, one of them holding a rifle on Tobin.

Silva fired, no doubt at the man on the bank whom I could not see, and kicking the door wide I dropped into the road and yelled, "Tobin! *Let 'em go!*"

The man with the rifle half turned to fire at me, and I let him have a barrel in the chest. Then wheeling, I fired at the second man.

Tobin, with a yell, cracked his whip at the third man and the frightened horses lunged into a run.

A bullet kicked dust at my feet, and I leaped for the brush, tripped over a root and fell headlong, clinging to my now empty shotgun.

I came up, six-shooter in hand, but there was nothing in sight except the body in the road. Breaking the shotgun, I plucked out the empty shells with my left hand, fed two cartridges into the barrels, and snapped the gun shut. I reholstered my pistol, and crouched, waiting.

It was very still. It was warm in the sun, but here in the partial shade of the pines it was cool. A lot of shooting had taken place, much of it lost in the confusion of my own actions, and I had no idea how Silva or Tobin Dixie had fared.

I was alone, on a mountaintop with a dead or wounded outlaw and his three companions.

Where were they? Silva had fired—several times, I thought, and he had been shot at. My first shot had nailed the man at the horse's head; my second shot had gone wild, but I might have gotten a few more shots that counted.

Ever so gently, I eased back, took one quick glance to see the way, and moved swiftly through the rocks and bushes in the direction the stage had taken.

From where I stopped I could survey the mountainside. It was brush-covered, with scattered pines toward the crest, pines that thickened into a forest lower down. The red bank from which Heseltine had spoken, and from which the rocks had been pushed to stop the stage, lay before me, about thirty yards off. On my left front was a white cliff of fractured rock that was fifty to sixty feet high. Brush grew along its base. I decided their horses must have been tied somewhere near the base of that cliff, which cut them off from the uphill direction.

To escape, if that was what they planned, they must go down the mountain on my left. As they would not be likely to take the stage road, they would probably try to get through the mountains by some prearranged route that must also be to my left.

But they might not try to escape. They knew I was here, and they knew I was on foot. They might try to kill me.

They must know the stage driver would send a posse back to look for me and to hunt for them. Would they try to put distance between them and the scene of the holdup? Or would they try to hunt me down?

I was crouching there in the hot sun when suddenly a voice called out: "Bob? King is dead."

My position was a good one, with a field of fire in every direction. Well down behind the rocks, I called out, "Bob? Reese? I want my money back!"

There was a moment of silence, then Heseltine's voice came. "Tucker, lay off, d'you hear? Lay off, or I'll come after you!"

"Come on, Bob. I'm right here, waiting—only bring my money when you come."

"You go to hell!"

"Scared, Bob? You were supposed to be the tough man. You get that money back to me, Heseltine, every cent of it, or you'll never rest another day as long as you live."

"Burnett," I yelled, "you're a fool to tie up with a man who'll be watched every minute. Any job you try to pull off will fail!

"We were waiting for you today, Pit. We knew you were coming. But I don't want you, I want my money.

Reese and Heseltine took it."

There was no answer, and I did not talk any more. I watched from my cover, but they did not come. Some distance off, I heard the pound of hoofs, and then silence.

I waited perhaps half an hour and then I moved, striking for a clump of boulders and the trees beyond. I heard no sound, no movement anywhere.

After a while I found tracks near the stage road and followed them. There were drops of blood here and there on leaves or grass. Near the white cliff I found where horses had waited.

They were gone.

Slowly, shotgun in hand, I plodded back. Birds were singing and the air was bright, but the afternoon was waning. At the scene of the holdup I found Burns King. He had taken my shotgun blast full in the chest, and must have been dead before he hit the ground.

Dragging the body to the side of the road, I waited. A posse would come, and perhaps the stage itself would return, its delivery made.

Of them all, Burns King deserved killing the least, I thought, but when a man starts out to break the law it is one of the risks he takes.

I was no nearer recovering my money. As a matter of fact, it was growing less likely all the time.

When I had been waiting more than an hour and had about decided to build a fire, a buckboard appeared, and then another. There were three men in one, four in the other, all armed. Do Silva was one of them.

We loaded King's body into a buckboard and I climbed in too. Silva had been shot through the upper arm at the first blast, had lost his grip on his rifle, and had only managed to get off a few shots.

He was angry with himself. He looked at me, and said, "You're game, *amigo.* You went right after them."

"I intended to. I still intend to. I want a horse, and when I get one I'm coming back and try to pick up their trail."

And that was the beginning of it, the beginning of six long months of riding, six months in which I stayed on their trail during every waking minute, six months in which I gave them no rest, no time to gather their forces or to spend the money.

To Animas City, to Farmington, to Socorro. There had been five hundred dollars on Burns King, and I used the reward money to follow the others. In Kingston I heard Pit Burnett had deserted them.

I came face to face with him in a saloon.

CHAPTER 11

He turned to face me as I neared the bar. He was unshaven and haggard-looking. "Is it me you're lookin' for?" he asked.

"No, Pit. I want your friends."

"They're no friends of mine. It was a sorry day that I met with them. I've left them, and good riddance."

"I'm sorry about King. It was the breaks of the game."

Burnett shrugged. "It could have been me. Or you. When a man takes gun in hand there is only one end to it, come soon or late." He glanced at me. "Is it after them you are?"

"Yes."

"I broke from them at Horse Spring." He jerked his head toward the west. "I doubt if they came to Socorro."

"Where's Ruby?"

"I'd not be knowing that, but Heseltine gave her money, quite a wad of it, and she left them and took the stage for Santa Fe."

"Did I get much lead into Reese?"

"A dozen or so buckshot into his hide, but no damage done except that he's scared. You've got him scared from his wits."

"What about Heseltine?"

"Nothing scares him. Nothing at all. But you've made it impossible for him to pull a job. You're always too close, and you give him no time."

He looked hard at me. "How long are you going to keep it up?"

"Until I have my money, or he's dead. Until both of them are dead."

Pit finished his drink, and I bought him another. "Thanks," he said. "You might say you owe me this much. I haven't made a dollar since you took after us."

"Broke?"

He grinned at me. "You betcha. This here drink was my last. I hoped to find a friend who would stake me."

"You have," I said. "I'll grubstake you." I put a twenty-dollar gold piece on the bar. "Take that, and do one thing for me."

He fixed his eyes on me. "And what would that be?"

"Stay away from them. I think you're a good man, Pit, and when I tangle with them I wouldn't like to find you in the way."

"You won't." He picked up the money. "I'm taking this as a loan." He turned toward the door, but stopped and came back. "Why should I cover for them? They brought me nothing but bad luck. So I'll tell you this.

"Ruby Shaw went to Los Angeles. She'll be registered at the Bella Union Hotel, and she'll wait for them there."

If Pit Burnett had left them at Horse Springs and they were now en route to Los Angeles, they had a good lead on me, and my horse was about used up. So I made a swap at the livery stable, giving a little to boot, and owned a strawberry roan mustang that took me down the trail toward Prescott.

It was a far piece, and a man had to ride with eyes for Apaches. They haunted the canyons of the Mogollons, alert for lone travelers or isolated cabins.

Angling north, I came on a company of freighters—twenty huge wagons, drawn by bull teams, and twenty-five men, including the cook, two wranglers, and the boss. I told them my name, and I shared their beans and beef, adding to the menu with three turkeys I'd killed shortly before. Around the fire there was good talk.

"Shell Tucker?" the cook said. He was a hard old man, who had been a buffalo hunter and a mustanger. "I know that name."

"I'm from Texas," I said.

"An' Colorado. I heard about you."

"There's not much to hear." I filled my coffee cup. "I'm headed for Los Angeles," I added.

"Is that where they've gone? I heard you was follerin' after them pretty constant."

When I said nothing the cook went on, "I heard about Bob Heseltine, and I know Burnett. He carries a derringer, too."

"Burnett's out of it. I saw him in Socorro."

"Kill him?"

"Why? He's left them, and he'd never done anything to me. It's Heseltine and Reese I want."

When I left them I went on my way toward Prescott.

The sun was low over Thumb Butte as I rode down Gurley Street and watered my horse in Granite Creek. My eyes had been busy as I came through town, but I saw no horses like the ones Heseltine and Reese had been riding when I last saw them.

There wasn't much activity in town. I took off my chaps and brushed the dust off my boots as best I could. The water in the horse trough did for a looking glass as I combed my hair. Then I hitched my six-gun into place.

Close by I found an eating place where they served you on red-checked tablecloths. There were a few coffee and grease stains left from earlier eaters, but that didn't seem to have any effect on my appetite.

There was a door to the kitchen, and eight tables, each with four chairs, and a long table with benches on each side. From where I sat I could look out on the street, but I could see only a piece of it.

It was still and cool there, and the room seemed to be waiting, as empty chairs and tables always seem to be waiting.

It was good just to sit there and relax. Out back somebody was singing an old Spanish song, with sentiment but with a bad accent. As I listened, my thoughts kept turning back to Vashti, to her father, to Con Judy, and all I'd left behind me.

What was I doing, anyhow? The chances were the money was mostly gone by now, gambled away or spent. I didn't have hatred for the men I followed, so much as a feeling that somehow justice must be done. My father might have been alive but for them . . . and me.

Months had passed since then. I had ridden away from home a gangling, know-it-all boy, and now I was a man, or what passed for one; but still I had no idea what I wanted to become, or where I was going . . . except to find Heseltine.

Was it really the money? I did want to pay those who trusted my father and me. Yet there was something more, I suspected. Those two had faced me over the money, and I had backed up. It was all right to say I had done the right thing, and the older I grew and the more I learned, the more I knew I had been wise beyond my years . . . but had it really been wisdom? Or had it been because I was afraid?

One more time, I told myself. One more time facing them to see if I had been afraid . . . and perhaps to convince them I wasn't.

Burns King was dead, but I would file no notches on my gun—that was a tinhorn's trick. Pit Burnett had chosen to pull out, perhaps because of my haunting their trail.

Suddenly I realized that I might destroy them in that way, without a gun. What if I stayed so close to them they had no time to plan? No time to prepare? I knew enough about such men to know that other outlaws would begin to avoid them, knowing that I was always around somewhere.

The cook for the freighters had known me. Perhaps that was my best weapon: just to let the story follow them, the story that no matter where they were, I was coming right behind them.

As I sat there I thought that Prescott was a pleasant place to be. I looked out on the darkening street and thought of the lights in the cabins along the hillsides and on the flat. Men were coming in from their chores, standing their rifles in the corner, hanging up their guns, sitting down at tables with their families.

Truth to tell, I was lonesome. What I'd like to do was sleep until sunup and then mount my horse and ride back to Colorado. Ride back to where I had friends, and to where Vashti was.

In the kitchen the cook was working over the dishes, and the girl who waited on tables was busy somewhere else. The restaurant was empty, lighted by four kerosene lamps with reflectors behind them, one lamp to each wall. My table was at the edge of one circle of light.

I ate slowly. The food was good, but I was so hungry it tasted better than it was.

A while back my head would have been full of fancies, wild stories in which I was always the hero, the man galloping up to save some girl in danger, or someone else in trouble. Right now my brain was still, with no fancies, no imaginings. But it was listening. For now I was a hunting man, and a hunting man never knows when he himself may become the hunted. I had some considering to do.

Why had Heseltine and Reese not gone with Ruby Shaw? If she was taking the stage, why had they chosen to ride horseback?

First, they might not have the money, but I had seen no signs of their spending.

Second, they expected to pull a job of some kind before reaching Los Angeles, to give them more money.

Third, they wanted to take care of me without waiting any longer. Perhaps they planned both to do another holdup and to get me, too. They had tried that at the house in the mountains, just as they had tried it in Leadville. I knew that I must be careful, always.

I'd made my first move against them in their attempted holdup of the stage. Pit Burnett left them after that; and word was likely getting around that to tie up with Heseltine and Reese meant trouble.

My meal was finished, but I didn't want to move. Down the street I could now hear the faint sounds of a music box, and once a horse walked down the street, but Prescott seemed peaceful.

The relaxation had allowed time for me to consider myself. The brief contact with Con Judy and his friends had, I realized, given me a new viewpoint, some new standards of behavior, some new ideas.

This country wasn't going to stay wild and free always. Folks would be moving in and cluttering it up, and although the wild, reckless men came first, they would soon be followed by people who wanted to be more settled, who wanted a peaceful community with churches, schools, and all of that.

There would be no place in such a world for men like Heseltine. Kid Reese might change, for he was a follower, a man who tried to fit himself in. He wasn't big enough to be a leader, so he chose a leader who was the kind he wanted to be, and lived in his shadow. In this case, he'd chosen the wrong man to pattern himself after, and it was going to get him killed. . . . Or in prison, which was much the same thing. Why a man would risk years of his life for a few quick dollars was beyond me.

Those two men had probably made the move to Los

131

Angeles as an attempt to get clear out of the country where I was, to leave me behind. If that failed they would likely try an ambush, and I could be sure they would be watching their back trail. Between here and the coast there was a lot of wide-open country where a lone rider could be watched.

A thought came to me. Suppose I outran them? Got ahead of them, and did some ambushing on my own?

Well, there was a way to do it. The stage. It would change horses often, and would make fast time, and I could be in Los Angeles before they arrived. So the stage it would be.

I stood up. Placing a quarter on the table to pay for my meal, I pushed open the door and stepped outside into the cool night.

"Tucker . . . ?"

I turned.

The man stood in the half-light from the restaurant window. He was a stranger, but a gun was in his hand.

Flame stabbed from the muzzle, something struck me, and I half turned. I was already holding my own gun in my hand. I could feel the bucking as I fired it.

I saw the man spin around and slam hard against the wall of the building. He was lifting his gun again.

The moment was like an hour. His gun came up, I felt the coolness of the breeze on my face, heard a door slam down the street, heard men running. There was in me an icy coolness. I had no idea why he wanted to kill me, but I knew this time what I had to do. I had to stop him.

My feet were spread wide, my gun was steady. I fired, and he threw both hands to his head and screamed. It was the last sound he ever made.

A man who wore a star grabbed my arm. "Here! What's going on here?"

The girl from the restaurant spoke. "Marshal, this man just finished his supper. He's been sitting alone, bothering nobody. The other man was waiting for him in the dark outside."

"He won't wait for anybody else," somebody said. "He's done for."

"This man's hit, too, Marshal. I saw him stagger."

I put my hand to my side. My watch—it had been pa's—was a mess of jagged metal. The watch, in my vest pocket, had stopped the bullet.

"I don't know the man," I said. "I never saw him before."

The girl from the restaurant spoke up again. "He's been around town for two or three days. Just as if he was waiting for somebody."

"Seems open and shut," the marshal said. "He laid for you, made his try, and you nailed him. We don't need to hold court to figure that out. What's your name, mister?"

"Shell Tucker."

"The man who's chasin' Heseltine? Looks to me like he figured to stop you, friend.

"Meanin' no offense, Tucker, are you ridin' on in the morning?"

"Yes."

"I'd appreciate that. Too many shootings in town make folks nervous."

A man who had been examining the dead man spoke. "Letter here, Marshal. This here is Al Cashion . . . you know, the one who was in that shootin' over to Holbrook. He was a bad one."

"He ain't no more." The marshal bent over and checked the dead man's pockets. "Five hundred dollars here, Tucker. Looks to me like he was paid to kill you . . . Heseltine must be really scared."

"He isn't," I said. "Reese must have paid this man. Or Ruby Shaw."

"It was Ruby," the marshal said. "Cashion used to hang out with her." He handed me the money. "Heard you were tryin' to get back what had been stole from you. This here's a piece of it."

"Thanks," I said.

It wasn't until I was in bed in the hotel that I started to shake. I lay there in the dark, wide awake, in a cold sweat.

That man had come at me right out of the dark, and I had killed him. I had drawn fast . . . but I'd been lucky, awfully lucky, I knew.

CHAPTER 12

The Bella Union's name had been changed to the St. Charles. As the other passengers got down from the coach I kept a watchout for Ruby Shaw. The last thing I needed was to be seen by her.

And if Bob Heseltine and Kid Reese had arrived before me, I wanted to see them at least as soon as they saw me.

There were four good hotels in Los Angeles, but I went to the best, the Pico House. My new black suit was dusty, but I looked very much the traveling gentleman when I signed the book and was shown to a room overlooking the Plaza.

One thing I had noticed was that nobody carried a gun in sight. So I took my Colt and shoved it down behind my waistband on the left side, butt to the right, but covered by my coat.

Once in my room, I had my clothes taken out to be brushed and sponged, and ordered bath water heated. Los Angeles was new to me, but on the stage there had been a drummer who knew the place well, and he was a talkative man, so I'd listened and learned a good deal about the place.

Even before that I'd heard it said that Los Angeles was one of the roughest towns in the West. In the twenty years from 1850 to 1870 there had been forty legal hangings, and thirty-seven lynchings by Vigilantes or the like. Many of the bad ones who had been run out of San Francisco by the Vigilantes there had come to Los Angeles, and the early lynchings took care of some of them.

It was a big town for me, almost sixteen thousand people, folks said. Alongside the Pico House they had built the Merced Theatre, an almighty impressive place, finished not long before.

The Plaza, with its fountain, was right below my windows, and it seemed to be the center of things. Keeping a lookout from there I would sooner or later see everybody in town. While I waited for my clothes to be returned I looked down from the window at the folks below.

Many were vaqueros, the Mexican cowboys who I'd heard were the greatest ropers and riders anywhere. Some of the Spanish men were regular dudes, with clothes the like of which I'd never seen, decorated with silver, and wide-bottomed pants slashed up the sides, with red, blue, or green showing in the slash. Most of their sombreros had fancy hatbands of snakeskin, woven beads or silver.

The streets were dusty, but the valley itself was green. The drummer had told me that the people of the town raised enough to feed themselves and ship a surplus to Mexico.

I saw no sign of Heseltine or Reese, and I thought it was likely I had arrived before them. But I did see Ruby Shaw.

A spanking new rig came into the Plaza suddenly,

drawn by a matched pair of black geldings driven by a Mexican who sat up in front, whilst in the back seat was a handsome blonde all gussied up to look a lady of class. And it was Ruby, all right.

I had no idea what it cost to ride in a fine outfit like that, but it wouldn't come cheap. It might be that Ruby had brought my money west and was living it up, but I couldn't see myself facing a woman. The fact was that Ruby, although she looked handsome and could act the lady when she wanted to, was a tough one, a very tough article, indeed.

Maybe I wasn't up to tackling Bob Heseltine, even though I planned on doing just that. But I knew I wanted no part of Ruby Shaw. A woman can always make a man look bad, and the best thing I could do was avoid any contact with her. That didn't say I couldn't keep an eye on her. In fact, that was what I had to do if I wanted to find the other two.

One thing I'd learned from Con Judy. A man should get himself in with folks, let them get to know him, so when a showdown came he wouldn't be judged too harshly.

Buffum's was the place. Of the town's 110 saloons, Buffum's was acknowledged to be the best, and the meeting place of folks from all over. If a man wanted to get acquainted, that was the place. But I knew enough not to accept too readily the first men I came in contact with. Often enough they were deadbeats cadging a free drink, or they were folks who didn't set well with the local people.

So to Buffum's I went, my suit now brushed and neat. From Con Judy I'd learned to dress better, and to conduct myself with some dignity.

At the bar I ordered a drink, meanwhile letting my eyes and ears take in the crowd. Almost as much Spanish was spoken as English, and with few exceptions the Mexicans were the most elegantly dressed.

All four of the town's leading hotels, the Pico House, the St. Charles, the Lafayette, and the United States were close together, and none of them more than a few minutes from Buffum's, so there were a good many out-of-towners aside from local residents and ranching people.

The bartender had a moment of quiet, and I said, "Quite a crowd."

"The usual." His eyes shifted to me. "You buying land?"

"Looking around. I'm interested in cattle. I might take a flyer in mining if there's a chance."

"That's a big gamble. There's gold out in San Gabriel canyon. A while back they were shipping twelve thousand dollars a month out of there."

He served a drink, then dropped back beside me. "They all come in here. The bigwigs, I mean. This is where the big deals are made."

"There are some beautiful girls around," I commented, "some of the prettiest I've seen."

"You betcha," he said, with sudden enthusiasm. "These Mexican girls are mighty pretty!"

"I saw one today that wasn't Mexican. At least, she didn't look it to me. A blonde, driving a pair of black geld—"

"Elaine Ross," he said. "She's at the St. Charles. She's a newcomer here, but she's sure cutting a wide swath among the menfolks. Two or three of the young dons are trying to court her, and Hampton Todd as well."

"Todd?"

"He's eastern. At least his pa was. They come out here together when Hampton was a boy. Fact is, I went to school with him. His pa was a widower, married a Mexican girl and fell heir to one of the big land grants, but he did right by her family. He made money and he spread it around.

"Fact is," the bartender added, "most of the Mexican families, the early ones, I mean, lost their land. Only those who had one of those New England boys marry into them, they kept theirs.

"There'd been no competition out here for years, and the Californios lived an easy, comfortable life. Money they took for granted sharing it around and spending it as if there was no end to it. Nobody was on the grab in those days, but when the Anglos began to come out, money-hungry and land-hungry, they grabbed everything in sight. It was a whole new way of thinking, and the Californios just weren't ready for it.

"Old Man Todd and some of the others, they took care of their folks, hung onto their lands, and as a result a lot of the old Californio families survived the rush.

"Hampton, he's a different cut from the old man. He's a big spender and likes to live rich. Looks to me as if he's got his eyes on Elaine Ross . . . and she's got money of her own."

"Well," I said carefully, "if she's only been here a short time, like that, maybe he should wait a bit and see what kind of a woman she is."

The bartender drew back, his eyes level. "Mister," he said, "I'll hear no man speak slighting of a woman."

Startled, I said, "I didn't speak slighting of her. Only that that's mighty short acquaintance, isn't it?"

He walked away from me and stopped down the bar, talking with some other men. After a moment, feeling the fool, I finished my drink and walked out.

What would they have thought if I had told them what I knew? They might have shot me. They had decided to believe what they wanted to believe, and the worst thing a man can do is to try to change an idea like that. But what would happen when Heseltine came to town? How would he like seeing his girl running with another man?

Outside, I strolled around the Plaza, watching the couples out for walks, and seeing several rigs go by. There were a dozen or so riders, men riding slowly by on handsome horses, their saddles loaded down with silver. Finally I went back to the hotel, lit my light, and tried to read. After a while I went to bed, and there in the dark wondered how long I'd have to wait.

For some reason I was restless, and it took a long time for me to fall asleep. Then suddenly, I was awake.

There had been no unusual sound . . . I was somehow sure of that, yet there I was, wide awake and staring into the darkness. For a moment I lay quiet, listening.

There was no sound from outside, which meant it was long after midnight, for the saloons took time to quiet down, and men going home often stopped in the Plaza to talk. Carefully, I eased out of bed.

Looking at the crack of light beneath the door I could see that no one stood there. Dim light from outside showed my small room clearly enough to see I was alone. I crossed to the window and, keeping well to one side, looked out.

For a moment all I could see was the Plaza, the shadows under the awnings across the streets, the faintly silver finger of water from the fountain. And then I heard horses.

Two riders—no, there were three. Three riders.

Waiting beside the window I saw them walk their horses into the Plaza, pausing almost beneath my window as they considered the hotel and talked in low tones. I could make out no details, but one of them turned his head slightly and I caught a glimpse of his face.

Kid Reese . . .

My wait was over then; they were here.

After a moment or so, they rode on, disappearing in the direction of Los Angeles Street.

Returning to my bed, I stretched out, pulled the covers over me, and began to think about the situation. Hampton Todd and Bob Heseltine . . . I'd keep out of sight and see what developed from that situation, but in the meanwhile I'd locate the outlaws' horses and the place where they chose to stay. So far as I knew, Heseltine was not well known here. Reese was certainly a stranger.

After some time I fell asleep, with nothing solved except to wait. There are some times when a man has to go in, guns a-blazing. There are others when it pays to just wait and see what develops.

At breakfast I saw Hampton Todd across the room. He glanced my way, his eyes level and cold. Now, what was that about? I'd never met the man. Paying strict attention to my food, I found myself feeling worried.

Ruby Shaw—or Elaine Ross as she called herself here—had a way with men. She might have seen me and, preparing for what might come, had told Todd some cock-and-bull story about me. Or the bartender might have said something.

Actually, I'd said nothing for anyone to take offense at, but the bartender had taken it badly, and so might others. I was going to have to stay away from Ruby Shaw, and I was going to have to move with care.

The first thing I did was to go to Wells Fargo and

send part of the money I'd gotten in Prescott to the folks back in Texas.

After arranging to send the three hundred dollars I figured was their share, I said to the agent, "If you wanted to sort of keep out of sight in this town, I mean if you were an outlaw, where would you go?"

He glanced at me. "Sonora Town. It's the Mexican end of town. There's Mexicans all over town, but they are mostly the ones who have been here for years. The drifters and the newcomers live in Sonora. There are a lot of good folks over there, but they mind their own business. There are a lot of bad ones there, too, and a man could go among them and they'd hide him."

He finished an entry in a book, put my money away, and then he said, "If it's anybody I should know about, it might help to tell me."

"Ever hear of Bob Heseltine? Or Kid Reese?"

He took some papers from a pigeonhole in his rolltop desk. "I've got a flyer on them. Suspected of a stage holdup."

"That's right. Does it say anything more?"

He glanced at the flyer. "Reported to be traveling with a woman, Ruby Shaw. A blonde, five foot three, one hundred and twenty-five pounds. . . ." He looked up. "You must be Shell Tucker. You were the stage-company agent."

"For a short time. Heseltine and Reese rode in last night, in company with another man."

"You are sure it was a man? Not the woman?"

I looked him straight in the eye. "It was a man. The

girl was already in town. She got here before I did."

He did not make the connection. "Well," he said, "if you need any help, you can come to us. That is, if you have a warrant."

"I haven't."

He shrugged. "There's not much I can do, then, except to put out some feelers. I have friends over in Sonora Town and they'll listen around. If I hear anything, I'll let you know."

I made one last attempt. "The girl will not be using her own name, I imagine, and won't be living over there. She likes to spend money and live high on the hog."

I surveyed the street with care. I pulled my hat-brim down and studied each face I saw, each window I passed. They had tried to kill me before, and if they so much as imagined I was in town, they would try again.

Had it been mere chance that they stopped under my window last night? What if Ruby knew I was in town and had somehow passed the word along?

As well as the outlaws in Sonora Town, there were others holed up in the canyons of the Santa Monica Mountains. While there were cattle on the hills, there were not nearly so many since the four-year drought that had ended in 1868. The cattle business in the vicinity of Los Angeles was, they told me, a thing of the past.

Suddenly I saw a man crossing the street toward me. It was Hampton Todd. He stepped up on the board-walk and stopped. "Are you Shell Tucker?" he asked.

"I am."

"I understand you have followed Miss Ross to this city. That you are persecuting her. Well, I want to tell you—"

"I do not know a Miss Ross," I interrupted.

"What?"

"I came here," I answered, "in pursuit of two outlaws and a woman friend of theirs, Miss Ruby Shaw. I do not know anyone named Miss Ross, nor do I have any interest in a person of that name."

Deliberately, I turned away and started down the street. I had taken only two steps when he was upon me. He took hold of my shoulder, and I turned swiftly, throwing his hand off.

"Keep your hands to yourself, Todd," I said. "I have no trouble with you, and I don't want any."

He glared at me, angry, but suddenly wary. He was wise enough to see I was ready for trouble if he wanted it.

"Leave her alone," he said. "Or I'll kill you!"

"Take my advice, Todd, and ask the Wells Fargo agent to see his flyer on Heseltine. Do that before you get yourself killed. And watch yourself. Heseltine is in town."

"What's he got to do with me? This . . . this Heseltine?"

"Look at the flyer," I said, and walked away from him.

"Go to hell!" he shouted after me.

CHAPTER 13

The last thing I wanted was trouble in Los Angeles, but Ruby Shaw had planted suspicion of me, and I doubted if Hampton Todd would examine the flyer. Nor would the Wells Fargo agent be inclined to speak up under the circumstances.

He had probably overheard the altercation in the street, as others had, but he had to live here and stay in business, and from his standpoint his best course was to know nothing one way or the other.

Hampton Todd was known and liked by many; he was disliked by some. But I was a stranger, and therefore suspect. The woman they knew as Elaine Ross was beautiful, and conducted herself as a lady.

There were many solid, able men in Los Angeles. From all I heard the town had been fortunate in many of its early settlers, for such men as John Temple, Abel Stearns, and Benjamin Wilson had come to build, not to make their money and get out. Most of these men would be friendly to the Todds, and I knew none of them.

It would be well for me to act with caution or I would find myself in trouble with people for whom I felt no animosity.

At the livery stable I collected my horse and rode slowly down Spring Street and out of town, taking the road west toward Rancho La Brea.

My best thinking was done when alone, and west of the settlement there were only a few scattered huts, clumps of oak trees, and in some areas, forests of prickly pear.[4] This was land where cattle had grazed until the drought had killed many of them and caused others to be slaughtered to save the hides and tallow. Farther west was the little town of Santa Monica, with visions of becoming a great port, to rival San Francisco. A railroad had been completed not long before that led from Los Angeles to Santa Monica, and a pier built to deep water where ocean-going vessels could dock.

As I rode I occasionally glanced back toward the pueblo, but I saw no one. It was a sunny, pleasant day. I could catch glimpses of sunlight on the sea, and in the distance I could see Catalina Island.

Several times I drew up just to look out over the vast panorama before me. Close on my right were the mountains, a low, rugged range covered with chaparral and split by occasional canyons that offered a way to San Fernando Valley beyond. There were grizzlies in those mountains, although there were fewer now.

My best bet, I thought, was to avoid Ruby Shaw and her new friends. Bob Heseltine and Kid Reese had ridden into Sonora Town and gone into hiding . . . no doubt they knew to whom they could go for shelter.

Along the slope of the mountain I found a wagon trail, no more than two ruts in the sparse grass, but it was a trail, so I followed it, and soon overtook a wagon with an old Mexican driving.

He lifted a hand to me and I slowed my horse to a walk. His smile was pleasant.

"It is a splendid view," I said, waving a hand at the wide expanse of grassland, oak clumps, and cacti that lay between us and the sea.

He drew rein and I stopped beside the wagon. "It is a thing to be seen," he said, "and always the light is different. I have looked many times from here, and"—he gestured toward the mountains—"from up there."

"I hear there are outlaws in the canyons," I suggested. "You are not afraid?"

He shrugged. "I am an old man, *señor,* and a poor one. Why should they bother me?"

"No man is poor," I said, "who can look on beauty. It lifts the spirit."

He glanced at me, then away. "You have come from far?"

"Texas," I said, "and Colorado."

"Ah, I know them. When I was younger, *señor,* I was a traveled man. You come here for land?"

"No," I replied, "I follow two men. They have taken what did not belong to them."

"You are a Ranger?"

"I am a man."

He nodded to indicate the road ahead. "My home is near. At this time of day I drink coffee. You will join me?"

Now, many people might have thought it a waste of time to talk with this old Mexican, but I had learned by now that no man's friendship is to be despised, and especially not by me, who had no friends here.

His house was small, an adobe that stood on a shoulder of the mountain. There was a small corral close by, and several burros, two horses, and a small flock of goats. The house was poor, but neat.

There was a young girl there, of sixteen or so, and a boy a couple of years younger.

"My grandchildren," he said. "They help me. It is good to have grandchildren when one is old."

"You had a son?"

"Three sons. One is in Mexico, and two are gone. They were vaqueros, *señor,* and the way of a vaquero is hard. One was killed when his horse fell with him after he had roped a wild bull. My son killed the bull, but the bull had a horn into him first. He was three days getting home, *señor,* and it was too late to help him."

"And the other?"

"The desert, *amigo.* The desert killed him, as it has killed others. At least, he went into the desert and he has not come back. Perhaps it was the Mohaves, for they had stolen horses from the ranchos. He pursued, separated from the others, and we have never found him. It was three years ago. If he could have come, he would have, for these children are his, and he was a good man, a good son."

We sat at a table inside the adobe and looked out through the open door. From where we sat we could look far across the low hills to where the sun glinted on the sea. Below us was the almost flat plain, and the cienaga with its marshy ground. He rambled on, talking of his family, of his life there, and of the country around.

And then he said, "These men you spoke of? They are gringos?" He hesitated, embarrassed. "I am ashamed. It is not a good word, gringo."

I smiled at him. "What is such a name? It is nothing. I do not mind at all. It is a convenient name. People should not allow themselves to be disturbed by such little things. Yes, the men are gringos."

My description of the men was as clear as I knew how to make it. The boy listened, too, and when I had finished he spoke in Spanish to his grandfather. Spanish was not new to me, for I had grown up in Texas, where half of our riders were Mexican. I knew what he said, but made no comment.

"My grandson says there are such men in Sonora Town. He has seen them. They live at the house of Villareal—or so he calls himself. He is a man who puts on names as he does shirts . . . and changes them more often."

"He knows where this house is?"

"He does know. He saw them only last night when he was at the house of a friend. They ride fine horses, and they leave their horses at the corral of Villareal. He has a cantina, *señor*."

A cantina in Sonora Town? "It is a tough place? I mean, is it a place where bad men get together?"

"*Si* . . . it is. You must not go there, *señor*."

It might mean a gun battle, more than likely with someone other than the men I wanted, and it would bring me no closer to the money that belonged to us.

"Could your son slip a message under the door without being seen? At night, perhaps?"

The boy nodded. "Of a certainty. I go sometimes to a store that is close by. I pass the cantina."

I wrote one line: *Tell Ruby Al Cashion was not good enough.*

If they did not know already, that would tell them that I was in town, and then they must hunt me down. I did not think they would be wise enough to wait to see what I might do.

Toward evening I rode back to town, but not by the trail I had left by. I rode down past the pits where Hancock's men were digging asphalt for roofs, skirted a few huts, and rode south to enter the pueblo from that side.

After stabling my horse I went back to the hotel, but I had just reached my room before there was a rap on the door. A moment I hesitated, and then spoke. "Who's there?"

"Sheriff Rowland. I'd like a word with you, sir."

He was a well-set-up man, with a mustache and chin whiskers, laugh wrinkles around his eyes, and a pleasant expression. I'd heard of him. He was a good man, and only a short time before had engineered the capture of the bandit, Tiburcio Vasquez.

"How do you do, Sheriff? I am Shell Tucker."

He was amused. "I know. That's what I've come to

talk to you about. You have business in the city?"

"I am looking for a place to settle, and this is a beautiful spot."

"I see." I indicated the rocking chair and he sat down. "I had word you were hunting a couple of men."

"Yes, two men who robbed me. They later tried to rob a stage on which I was riding shotgun."

"I had not heard of that." He frowned. "What is your official capacity?"

"I do not have any. I'm acting to recover money they stole from me months ago."

"You believe they still have it? You are optimistic, sir."

"I am sure they still have it, or most of it. I haven't given them time to spend it."

Then I explained, telling all the events from the original loss of the money . . . the death of my father, and my meeting with Con Judy.

"I know of him. He has been here, discussing some railroad construction."

I could see that the name had carried weight, and I mentioned a couple of others I had met.

"You make my task difficult." He paused. "You see, sir, we cannot have strangers coming into town who are apt to cause trouble. I won't have gunfights here. There's been too much of that in the past, and the new people who are coming out to settle here want law and order. I am afraid, sir, that I must ask you to leave town."

"Did Hamilton Todd have anything to do with your decision?"

He did not care for that. He gave me a sharp look. "I make my own decisions, young man. Yes, he did lodge a complaint. Miss Ross told him you were following her, that you had caused trouble for her family."

"I will leave, Sheriff. In fact, I think the men I am following will also leave, but I suggest you go to the stage office and check the flyer they have on the men I am following, and on the woman who has accompanied them."

He stared at me. "You mean there's a notice out on those men?"

"Yes. And the woman is mentioned . . . and described." I hesitated just a moment. "Mr. Todd is a young man . . . Ruby Shaw is very attractive, and very shrewd. And she is a skilled actress."

"Who are these men you are following?"

"Bob Heseltine and Kid Reese."

Rowland was startled. "*Heseltine?* In Los Angeles?" He stood up suddenly. "I had no idea—" He looked at me again. "You're sure?"

"He was in Sonora Town last night. At Villareal's place."

Rowland was a good man, a strong man and an honest one. He had looked upon me as a potential troublemaker, which in one sense I was. That he knew who Heseltine was, was obvious.

"I have done my best to quiet the town, Mr. Tucker.

And understand, I want no trouble here."

"I understand. I'll certainly leave." I hesitated. "However, Sheriff, I'll not go far; and if I were you, I'd check that flyer. It might save you trouble."

"What do you mean?"

"Ruby Shaw is Heseltine's girl. Maybe they are now in a scheme together, to bilk somebody out of money. If they're not, and Heseltine should get the idea that Todd is moving in on him, Heseltine might become very abrupt. Make no mistake—he's a fast man with a gun."

He left me and I turned in, lying awake a long time, listening to the sounds from the Plaza and from the hotel itself. Rowland's call had not turned out badly. He would not want Heseltine in town, and if my note did not start them moving, Rowland would.

As for Hamilton Todd, I was through with him . . . or so I believed.

CHAPTER 14

Was I a fool to continue the pursuit? Was the money gone? Or had they cached it somewhere? Pit Burnett had said Heseltine had given Ruby Shaw a wad of money when she took the stage for Los Angeles. Was that what she was using to hire the fancy outfit she had?

It would not be unlikely for a girl like Ruby Shaw to come here with marriage in mind. There were too few pretty women in any town, and blondes were scarce. She was shrewd and knew her way around men, and a marriage with Hampton Todd might seem a nice outlook for a girl with her background.

Did Heseltine know what was going on? In such a small community there would be few secrets, and Villareal might have warned him of what was going on between Todd and Ruby Shaw—or Elaine Ross, as she now called herself.

Awakening in the last cold hour before the dawn, I found myself filled with a sort of dread. Suddenly I wanted nothing so much as to be out of this town. What inspired the feeling I did not know, but I was never one to buck my instincts.

Only a few minutes were necessary to pack my things and belt on my gun. Downstairs I went through the empty lobby, paused to look along the street where daylight was just beginning.

The street was empty, the Plaza was empty. I crossed the street and walked quickly along it toward the livery stable, my boots echoing on the sidewalk.

It was shadowy inside the livery stable, with only a faint glow from the lantern. In the stall my horse nickered and I saddled up, swung my saddlebags into place, and thrust my Winchester into the boot.

The horse was the rented one I had ridden before. Having come west on the stage, I no longer had a horse of my own, a situation that must be remedied at once.

Mounting, I turned the horse into the dusty street

and rode quickly down Main Street. Water trickled in the *zanja*. Under a couple of slender eucalyptus trees, and partly screened by clumps of century plant, I pulled off the street and looked back the way I had come.

A wagon with a double sprinkler was laying the dust on Main Street. It was the only thing in sight. I was now where the houses were more scattered, and soon I would be turning into the road that followed what had once been an Indian trail[5] leading west toward Santa Monica, but though I watched for several minutes, I saw no one.

There were groves of oranges, walnuts, and olives near where I waited, as well as further along, but they were poor places of concealment, so why was I so jumpy?

Abruptly, answering to instinct, I turned off the traveled way and rode down a dusty lane between two rows of orchards, past several of Holloway's Patent mills, and into a patch of prickly pear, crossed and crisscrossed by horse trails.

Once more I stopped, watching from hiding to see if I was followed. Riding into the prickly pear, I crossed a knoll and could see far ahead of me the cienaga, ten miles long by several miles wide over much of its area. The grass grew green there even in the driest weather, for most of that stretch was sub-irrigated.

By a roundabout route I rode back to the old Mexican's home. He saw me coming, and walked out to greet me. "Come, *amigo,* come inside! There is coffee."

I tied my horse at the corral, and followed him into the adobe. It was cool inside, and the view from the door was good. Any rider approaching could be seen for some distance.

The boy came in. "The men you seek are gone," he said. "I saw them find the paper I left, and when they read it there was argument. Later they brought out their horses and they rode from town, but Villareal did not go."

"I am not interested in him."

"But he is interested in you. He went to the livery stable looking for a roan horse, and then he asked many questions. He knows what horse you ride, *señor.*"

"I shall not ride him any more. I want to buy a horse, a good one, a tough one."

"There are many here," the old man said. "Since the cattle have become so few there are many horses. I will find you one."

"Is there a way down from the mountain behind us? Some way that Villareal might know?"

The old man shrugged. "There are ways, but he will not come close." He gestured. "I have guinea hens, and they are very alert. If anything strange moves they set up a fearful noise."

We had guinea hens in Texas, and I knew there was no better alarm, for they were more alert than even a good watchdog. And they were scattered over the yard here and along the mountainside, feeding.

The old man saddled a horse and rode away, and I sat by the door, watching the vast open space before me. The valley in which Los Angeles lay was fifty miles long by twenty wide, and from where I sat, much of it could be seen. Like the Pico House where I had stayed, the town was lighted by gas.

Conchita, the old man's granddaughter, brought me fresh coffee, some tortillas, and beans, placing them on a table beside me. Glad of somebody to talk to, she spoke of the town and the people. She was a bright girl, very much aware of her town and of California.

"Do you read, Conchita?"

"Yes. My mother taught me to read. She taught all of us—papa, too."

"She was Spanish?"

"No, she was an Indian. She was a Chumash."

"The ones who built the red boats? And who went to Catalina and the Channel Islands?"

"Yes. They lived sometimes there, sometimes on shore. My mother's people lived up the coast near Malibu." We talked of the area, of her people, and of Los Angeles. From time to time I would get up and look around, for I wanted no one coming close to me unbeknownst.

"The men of business are Irish or German, most of them," she said. "Mr. Downey is the richest man, I think.

"We are poor people, *señor,* but we live very well

here, for there is game in the mountains, and we raise our own vegetables. My grandfather has cattle, and some horses. Sometimes on Sundays we go to the Washington Gardens in Los Angeles, or to Old Santa Monica, to swim. We like the old town best."

She was leading up to something, and not just talking at random, for I had noticed that she was a young lady of purpose, rarely given to idle talk or wasted motion.

"Señor," she said suddenly, "if you wish to remain close there is a cabin in the canyon nearby. It is higher up than this. My father built it, for one day he hoped to live there. It is a place no one knows, and if you wished to stay there and watch, it could be arranged."

"I have men to follow," I said doubtfully, "and I must find them."

"They will come to you, *señor.* Villareal looks for you, and it is not for himself. I think when he finds you he will tell them."

The vague, haunted feeling stayed with me. I had an idea I had been followed, even though I had seen no indication of it. Perhaps they had traced my actions on my previous ride . . . a few inquiries might have done that, for almost no one moves entirely unseen. People are curious, wondering at strangers, or curious about anyone who is seen at unlikely times or in unlikely places.

I did not want to endanger my friends. "This place you spoke of, Old Santa Monica?" I asked Conchita. "It is near the sea?"

She explained that the trail to the plateau would take me there. The carriages would stop at Old Santa Monica Corral and at Frank's Saloon, a large pavilion with a rustic porch running across the front. There was a brook nearby and a clump of alders.

For another hour I waited, and then the old man returned leading a line-back dun, with legs black to the knee, and black mane and tail.

"Seventy dollars," he said, "and it is cheap."

When evening came to the valley below, and when lamps were being lit in the scattered houses, I said my good-byes and rode down the slope through the brush, turned off the trail, and cut across the grassland, losing myself in the shadows. It was chill, for when the sun goes down in that country the cold air comes, as it came now.

The dun went with a long, easy stride. Westward I rode, across the darkening plains, down the slope of the long hill and across the wide pastureland, until I could see the Santa Monica road, white in the moonlight, but I avoided it, holding to the north of it until the lights of the town were close.

I felt sure there would be little about the area that Villareal did not know. I rode over the plateau and down to Old Santa Monica, where there were lights in Frank's Saloon, and the sound of the surf along the beach. Dismounting at the corral, I tied my horse, and waited there in the shadows, letting my ears get used to the rustle of the leaves, the movements of the sea, and the sound of voices from the saloon. Only then did

I cross the hard-packed clay of the yard and go up the steps to the wide porch.

There were half a dozen people in the saloon, several drinking at the bar, and two who sat at a table nearby with a bottle of country wine.

The table I chose was at one side, on the edge of the light. I sat down, put my hat on the chair beside me, and soon a waiter came over to my table.

When I had ordered a meal and coffee, I began to relax. It was an easy, pleasant place. The talk was friendly, and I sensed at once that it was a good place to be.

Frank—I supposed it to be Frank—came to my table. "You wish to stay the night? I have rooms," he said.

"I would."

He glanced at the pistol in its holster. "You will not need that here, my friend. We are a friendly people."

"I am sure." I smiled at him. "I do not carry it for you or your people," I said, "but for others who may come along."

"You have enemies?"

"Doesn't everyone? Yes, as a matter of fact, I do. But tonight I want only to rest and listen to the sea, to eat a good dinner, to drink coffee, and to wait. Tomorrow? It is another day, and when tomorrow comes I shall go over the mountain, I think, or follow some of the Chumash trails toward Ventura."

"You know about the Chumash? They were a good people, and a daring people. There are caves in these mountains with their paintings. I have found many myself. They were not such a simple people as some would have you believe. Their lives, yes, and their customs were simple, but not their thinking."

When he had gone I ate and listened to a girl singing somewhere out of sight, a pleasant old song in Spanish.

Soon, after a good dinner and several cups of coffee, I was thoroughly at ease. So much so that when the stranger walked in I scarcely noticed him. Not, at least, until his face turned toward me.

It was Doc Sites.

CHAPTER 15

His eyes met mine across the room, and for a moment he remained still. His fingers were on the bar-edge, his body close against it. I did not want to kill him, and to draw against me he must move back from the bar and turn. For the moment the advantage was mine.

"How are you, Doc? Looking for me?"

He had difficulty saying it, but he finally got it out. "No," he said hoarsely, "no, I ain't. I'm lookin' for them. They cut out and left me. They took it all."

"They aren't going to keep it, Doc."

"You're damn right they ain't! I'm goin' to find them, and—"

"Find who?" It was Bob Heseltine. He stepped in out of the darkness, a gun in his hand.

Behind me Kid Reese spoke. "An' you set still, Shell, or I'll—"

Frank had a double-barreled shotgun in his hands and it was covering Heseltine. "Your fight is your own, and I want no part of it, but if you fire that pistol I'll knock you right off those steps. I just mopped this floor, and blood is hard to get up."

I tilted on the balls of my feet, clearing three legs of the chair off the floor and spinning on the other. I turned low and hard, swinging my arms wide. One of them struck the Kid's wrist and knocked his arm over and I came up, driving into him with all my strength.

He was slim and wiry, not as strong as I was by a good bit, and my attack had taken him by surprise, his attention drawn by the bartender's sudden challenge of Heseltine. He staggered back, and I slugged him hard in the wind, my left hand gripping his gun wrist. The gun went off into the floor and I hit him again.

He lost his grip on the gun and I turned loose with both hands. I had never realized how much I wanted to hit Kid Reese. He had always treated me with contempt, and I had always known he despised me but I had not wanted to admit it.

My blows were not only for him, but for the fact that I had once been stupid enough to want to be like him. I smashed him again and again in the face and the body until he sagged to the floor, blood dripping from a broken nose, his cheek ripped open by a blow.

Then I turned sharply around. Heseltine, his gun in

hand, was standing very still, Frank's shotgun held steady on his belt buckle. No man in his right mind, and especially not such a gun-canny man as Heseltine, wanted to tackle a shotgun at twelve feet.

"He's supposed to be very good, Frank," I said. "Let him holster his gun and then turn him loose. I want to see how good he is."

"Nothing doing." Frank's voice was casual. "I have no part in your troubles. I want no shooting in here."

He gestured with the muzzle. "You there! Shove that mouse back into its hole. Then you back out of here, get on your horse, and ride out. One wrong move and I'll cut you in two.

"In case you want to know, by this time, my cook is settin' by the back door with a Winchester, and he'll have you dead in his sights from the moment you step outside. You ride out of here, and I don't give a damn where you go, but get out."

"As for you"—he spoke to me without turning his head—"you ride right after him . . . and don't come back here wearing a gun. Now start moving."

Bob Heseltine backed toward the door. There he stopped. "You'll get your chance, Tucker. I'll see to that."

"Thanks, Bob," I said. "I've been wondering why you were ducking me. Your friend Al Cashion couldn't do your dirty work for you. I figured when you sent him you'd lost your nerve."

"Lost my nerve? Why, you—"

"Move!" Frank yelled at him. *"Now!"*

Heseltine vanished through the doorway and I turned slowly to look at Kid Reese. He was on his hands and knees now, blood dripping in slow drops from his nose.

Doc Sites was still standing at the bar. He had held very still, his hands on the bar, his face dead white. He was scared . . . scared stiff.

"Thanks, Frank," I said. "I'll be leaving."

"Don't thank me. Just get out. This here is a decent place. I want no shooting."

"Let these two go together," I suggested. "They deserve each other."

With that I stepped out into the darkness, listening to the fading sound of Heseltine's horse's hoofs. For a moment I waited in the shadows, then crossed swiftly to the corral and pulled the drawstring on the slipknot with which I had tied my horse.

I swung into the saddle, and turned up the coast. I had no intention of following Heseltine into the dark and into a possible ambush. Right now I wanted to get away. The sudden flurry of fighting with Kid Reese had taken a lot of the animosity out of me.

As for Doc Sites, I had nothing to do with him. He had been shot, he had evidently been robbed by his former companions, and he would suffer enough. What would happen between him and Kid Reese I neither knew nor cared. The thing I wanted was my money.

Suddenly, I wondered . . . where was that money? Who had it now? Ruby Shaw? She had some, perhaps, but not all. I could not believe Heseltine would be so gullible.

Turning my horse into deeper darkness, I rode with caution, seeking the white line of a trail that led along the plateau and through the brush and clumps of pin oak. And then I knew what I would do, and I circled and rode hard for the hills above the La Ballona ranch.

As I rode it came to me what I had done. Only a few minutes before I had challenged Bob Heseltine to a shoot-out! *I* had done that.

Conchita put her head out of the window as I rode into the yard. Yes, I could have a horse. Her grandfather was gone; only her brother was here. Swiftly, I swapped horses and rode out of the yard and down the trail toward Los Angeles.

When I rode down the street, across the Plaza, and into Sonora Town, it was nearly two o'clock in the morning. I knew the house to which I was going, and I dismounted in the shadows of an alleyway nearby. Heseltine might be here, but the chances were he had not yet returned—if, indeed, he was coming back at all.

Villareal's house was dark. It was a small adobe with a porch across the front and a backyard with a board fence around it. There was a stable with a door opening to the alley.

Stepping into the stable door I stood at one side, my hand on my gun, waiting and listening.

The horses rolled their eyes at me. There was a smell of hay, of horse manure, and of sweat. I eased

166

across the barn, speaking softly to the horses. One of them snorted a little, not loudly, but I spoke again and the horses continued with their chomping of hay.

I touched each one as I passed . . . and the last of the four horses was damp with sweat. It had been hard ridden, and not rubbed down.

Heseltine? Or Villareal?

I started to move on when a faint gleam from the back of the farthest horse drew my attention. It had been the first horse I had touched, when my eyes were not yet used to the darkness. I had merely put a hand on the horse's hip in passing.

Now I saw something I had not seen before. That horse was saddled.

I went back along the space behind the stalls and stepping into the last one I spoke to the horse, then patted it dry and cool. My hand went to the saddle, feeling the blanket. The blanket was damp.

I paused, listening. Somebody had ridden back here, riding hard. That somebody had swapped his saddle from the hard-ridden horse to a fresh horse and was evidently planning to leave at once.

He had gone into the house for something. For what? For his gear? For food and a canteen? Or for those things, and the money as well?

Glancing around quickly, I looked for a hiding place. The stalls were divided merely by poles that were waist-high, running from the wall to posts that supported the barn roof. I did not want to endanger the horses. The only place seemed beside the door.

As I turned to start for it the barn door opened, and there was a man with a lantern in one hand, a gun in the other. Over his shoulder was a pair of heavy saddlebags.

My own gun slid into my hand. "You can drop that gun," I said quietly.

Light from the lantern reflected from silver conchas on the shotgun chaps. It was Villareal.

"No," he said.

"I do not want to shoot you, but the money is mine."

"But I have it," he replied as quietly as I had spoken.

"A dead man does not spend money," I told him.

"Nor does a dead man carry money away. You can die as well as me."

"Both of us can die," I agreed, "or both of us can live. You want the money for what it can buy you in Mexico. But you know and I know that Bob Heseltine will follow you for it, and then he will kill you . . . if not, you will live in fear from now on.

"If I take the money you will be as you were. You will be here. You will have what you have had, and you will have no fear."

For a moment I paused, and then I added, "I think I want that money more than you do. I think I might die to get it, but I do not believe you want to die to keep it.

"In death," I added, "there are no pretty women. There is no tequila, no food, no good horses, no sunshine or rain. A little money lasts a very short time, but death is for always."

"You are a philosopher," Villareal said.

"I am a man who has been robbed, a man who feels a debt to the poor men to whom this money belongs." Quietly, there in the dark, holding the gun in my hand, I told him of the hard-working men down in Texas, the children who must go to school, the wives who needed shoes, the hard times all must face.

"I see," he said quietly. "I did not know from whom the money had been taken."

"I have followed Heseltine for many months," I said. "My father has died because of this money. Doc Sites was shot and seriously wounded because of it. Al Cashion was killed, and another man too. As long as I live I shall follow him."

He dropped his gun into his holster. "I am a bad man, *señor*, but not so bad as to rob the poor. Take the money. Only a little of it is here. The girl has it."

He handed me the saddlebags, and I took them warily. "Thank you, *amigo*," I said. "The men to whom this money belongs will speak well of Villareal. I shall tell them of your courtesy, and that you are a *caballero*."

"Gracias," he said. "And now, if you will permit?"

Backing from the door, he closed it behind him. Saddlebags in hand, I went out the other door, crossed to my horse, and rode back toward the Plaza.

I was coming from a street into the Plaza when suddenly I drew up.

It was Hampton Todd, and he had a rifle on me. "All right, where is she?" he demanded.

"Who do you want?"

"I want that damned girl, and you know where she is, damn you! Tell me, or I'll cut you down!"

"I wish I knew where she is," I replied calmly. "I have been looking for her, and for the man she rides with."

"You're that man! You know where she is, and I want her. And I want my money."

"*Your* money?"

"My money!" He shouted it at me. Windows were opening. His fury was attracting attention, but it did me no good. The man was trembling with rage, and he was ready to fire. At the slightest move, he would, and at that range he could scarcely miss.

"I do not know where she is, or what was between you." I kept my voice even. "I do not deny that I followed her here, looking for the man who robbed me."

"A likely story. There was no other man—*you* were the one!"

"Put the rifle down," I said, "and we can talk. The man you want is the man I want. And where he is, the woman will be."

"No!" He lifted the rifle again. "Tell me, or I'll kill you!"

I felt the *whap* of the bullet past my ear. I saw him jerk as I heard the report. His own rifle exploded, and the bullet missed me only by inches, and then he was staggering, falling.

"He killed me!" He spoke the words loudly and clearly, pointing at me. And then he rolled over into the dust. Men were running. Somebody yelled, "Get a rope!" Sheriff Rowland was suddenly beside me. "All right," he said. "Get off that horse."

"Sheriff, before I move I ask you to check my rifle and my pistol. You will find that neither one has been fired."

"What are you trying to say?"

"Don't listen to him, Rowland!" The man who spoke had obviously been drinking. His face was red and ugly-looking. A dozen other men were around him. "Hamp named him—pointed right at him!"

"Please, Sheriff," I said quietly.

He drew my Winchester from the scabbard. The barrel was cold, it held a bullet, the chamber was loaded. One by one he ejected the cartridges.

"As you see," I said, "the rifle has not been fired. Now the pistol, before anybody touches it, including me."

He threw a hard look at me, but he did check the pistol, too. He held it to the light and looked through the barrel. The cylinder held five cartridges, a sixth chamber was empty, but that was the way we carried them.

"These guns have not been fired." Rowland spoke clearly, emphatically. "This man could not have fired the shot."

An angry sound rose from the men around us, but as the information circulated among them, it died down.

"Then who did shoot him?" Rowland demanded.

"Somebody behind me, Sheriff," I said. "Somebody

who must have been in a second-story window, or on a roof, for the bullet passed me, but killed him, and he was standing on the ground."

The sheriff turned and looked across the Plaza. "Gone now, whoever it was. Question is, were they shooting at you or him?"

"At me," I said, "although Todd was about to take a shot at me himself. I was trying to talk him out of it."

"Get down and come inside," he said. "We've got some talking to do."

A deputy had come up and Rowland turned and spoke rapidly. The deputy hurriedly named five or six men in the crowd, and they scattered in the direction from which the shot seemed to have come.

Inside the Pico House we were away from the crowd, and Rowland led me into the hotel office. "Sit down," he said. "I want the whole story."

So I laid it out for him from the beginning. My pursuit of Heseltine, Reese, and Ruby Shaw, my discovery of her using another name here, Hampton Todd knowing some man was involved with her, and believing it was me.

"Why you?"

I shrugged. "I was probably the only one who seemed to know anything about her. I doubt if he ever saw Heseltine, so when he discovered another man was involved he thought it was me. I was a stranger in town, who knew her."

"You think it was Heseltine who fired the shot?"

"Heseltine or Reese, shooting at me. My guess

would be Heseltine. I don't think Reese was in any shape to be shooting at anybody, and I doubt if he would have been able to get here in time. Bob Heseltine could have."

"But he's a gunfighter, not a back-shooter."

"I've been dogging him, Mr. Rowland. I've been right on him. He can't find anybody to work with him because I'm always right there, not far behind him. Nobody wants to try pulling a job when somebody is hunting them before they start, and they don't want to get involved."

He considered the matter, taking a cigar from his vest pocket. "Have you ever thought of something else? It might have been Ruby Shaw who tried to kill you."

"Well," I said, "as nearly as I can find out, she was the one who hired Al Cashion."

"What do you know about that woman getting money from Todd?"

"Nothing at all, but she's shrewd and she's tough. There probably isn't a crooked dodge she doesn't know. He was roped in, and she might have spun him any kind of a story. Men like to brag . . . maybe he showed her how much cash he had. That would be like showing a hen to a hungry fox."

He got up. "There's no reason to hold you, but what I said before goes double. I want you out of town."

"Thanks, Mr. Rowland. A less reasonable man, and I might have been hung out there." I held out my hand.

"They're a rough crowd," he admitted, shaking my

hand. "There's a few among them I want to float out of Los Angeles the first chance I get. This town wants peace."

The Plaza was empty again. The light of dawn was yellow in the gray sky, with here and there a crimson streak. I liked the smell of the air, for the wind was from off the sea. I untied my horse and stepped into the saddle.

Rowland's deputy came back across the Plaza alone. He took a cigar from his mouth. "It was a woman," he said. "Went into an empty room. We could smell the perfume in there, and when she ran she forgot a glove."

He showed it to me. It was for a small hand—a hand that could pull a trigger as well as a man's could.

"See you," I said, and rode out of town.

They were gone again, lost again, out in the open again.

Where would they go?

CHAPTER 16

Conchita was in the yard when I rode up, and she came over to me as her grandfather came out of the house.

"You are well?" Her eyes searched my face. "A man passing by said there was a shooting in town."

When I had loosened the girth I went into the house with them. Conchita put coffee on the table and her brother came to listen as I told them what had happened.

"And now *amigo?*" the old man asked.

"I shall ride on. Try to pick up the trail."

He looked at me thoughtfully. "I am an old man, *señor,* and you must forgive me, but do you not think you waste your life? Those who lost the money have given it up now; they work and think of other things. Their lives go on, as yours must also.

"It does no good to follow and follow these men. They will have their suffering. Believe me, this woman will bring evil upon them. Such a woman will never cease from evil, and those with her will suffer. Leave them to their lives, *señor,* and find a place for yourself. The years pass swiftly, you will be an old man, with nobody, and with nothing to look back upon but the chase."

"It is something I must do. Sometimes I think that, just as a beaver must build dams, I must pursue these men."

"But all is changing around you. Even I, who am an old man, see that change. From day to day the law grows stronger. Men will work together, *señor,* and the lawless will soon be pursued wherever they may go."

He was right, of course. Sitting there in the cool room, I could look out on the sunlit yard and far away to the hills that bordered the sea. It was pleasant here, and there was land to be had. This valley was so beautiful it would attract people, and they would come and build homes here. It was the way of the world that nothing remains the same.

"I shall go on," I said. "I have a little more of the money, and I shall send it back to my neighbors."

We talked long, drank good coffee, and then with the morning gone, at noontime I tightened the cinch and stepped into the saddle. They stood in the open, on the hard-packed ground, and waved a good-bye. When I turned at last in my saddle to look back from the trail, only Conchita was still there. She lifted her hand once more, and I answered with mine.

Was it to be always so—that I should come into the lives of people, get to feel close to them, and then ride on? Would there be no end to it?

For two weeks I cast back and forth, trying all the trails that led out of Los Angeles to the east, the north, the south.

Then finally at a wayside station in the desert a man heard me speak of them and turned to me. "I saw some folks looked about like you said. A pretty blonde woman and two men. They came into Whiskey Flat from the southwest. They headed east out toward Walker's Pass."

We talked a little longer, and I knew he had seen them, all right. One of the men, he said, had a bad cut over his eye and another on his cheekbone. The other man, who was powerfully built, was wearing a leather coat and a black hat.

He drew me a map in the dirt outside the station, showing me Whiskey Flat, the trail to Walker's Pass, and our own location. We were at the new railroad town of Mohave. It had been called a lot of things before that. Elias Dearborn had a stage station there as early as 1860, and later the Nadeau freight teams used to make stops there.

"The trail here," the man said, "goes up through Red Rock Canyon toward Walker's Pass. It ain't much of a trail, but I come down that way yesterday, and you've got you a good horse. Carry plenty of water, though, and watch for rattlers. Seems to be a lot of them out this year."

"Pack horse?" I queried.

The man shrugged. "Not much chance here. Horses are scarce. Chavez and his outlaws—he's got the ragged end of the old Vasquez crowd trailin' with him—they've stole most of the good horses around. You might pick up a mule."

I went on, and I found the trail hot and dusty. When I had been riding about two hours it had become so hot that I knew it would be foolish to go on. I reined over to one side and rode into a small canyon where there was an island of shade forty or fifty feet across. Stepping down from the saddle, I poured a little water into my hat and let my horse drink, then tied him to some brush and settled down against the canyon wall to rest.

It was very still. My horse nibbled at brush, then closed his eyes and dozed three-legged, flicking his tail at an occasional fly.

From where I sat I could see almost half a mile of the trail as it wound up into the canyon that led to the plateau beyond. A lizard came out on a rock and studied me, his mouth gaping.

It was a place in which to sit and think about my own place in what was happening. One fact kept nudging me . . . I wasn't getting anywhere. Was my pursuit of Heseltine just a way of not looking forward to the future? All the time they were running and I was following, the fact was staring me right in the face that a man may run all his life and get nowhere.

The trouble was I'd just never had a destination in mind that I wanted . . . and yet I did want one. As long as pa had been alive I could think about being on my own, but postponing everything until that day when I would face the world alone. Then suddenly he was dead and I had those people to repay; and chasing Heseltine was just one more way of avoiding the day when I had to do and be all those big things I'd told myself pa was keeping me from doing and being.

With hat slightly tipped over my eyes, I watched the heat waves dancing, watched the trail as it went up through the rocks, where occasional ocotillo and some stunted Joshuas grew.

All right, I said to myself, supposing you get all that money back from Heseltine, what will you do then? Was I going to be a rancher? Was I going to try gold mining?

There were a lot of things I hadn't education enough to do, but even as I thought of that I could feel Con Judy's eyes on me and hear his dry comment. "You can read, can't you? If you can read, you can learn. You don't have to go to school to get an education, although it is the best way for most of us, and anyway, all school can give you is the outline of the picture. You have to fill in the blank places yourself, later."

That was what he would say, or something like it. The truth was that I had to face up to myself. Maybe pa had never gotten anywhere, but he never quit trying, and no matter how much he got beat down he kept on getting up.

There isn't any bright, patent-leather world that's always shining, no matter what you do . . . you have to make your own world, and your own place in it.

For the first time I checked the money in the saddlebags. There was slightly more than twelve hundred dollars. I'd keep a couple of hundred, and send the rest back to Texas.

After a while, I dozed. My horse awakened me, blowing softly.

I sat up abruptly. My horse's ears were pricked, and he was looking along the trail. A man was coming along it on a crow-bait horse. He was looking my way.

Getting up from the ground, I tightened my cinch. The shadows were reaching out from the rocks and cliffs. The sun was low, not yet down, but the coolness had begun and I could now ride on, but I was not pleased by this meeting.

The man on the crow-bait had pulled up on the trail, waiting for me. His hands were in plain view, and he showed no danger signs, but I was wary.

Swinging into the saddle, I walked my horse down to the trail.

"Howdy!" His eyes were a watery blue, but there was a sharpness to them, and I was sure he had missed no detail of my outfit. "Travelin' fur?"

"Walker's Pass. Maybe east from there."

"Ain't no other way to go, onct you get there."

"I could turn around and ride back," I said. And if there were no tracks there, that was just what I might do.

"So you could." His eyes clung to the saddlebags. "Been minin'?"

"Me? I'm a cowhand." And then I added, not too honestly, for I did not want him to know too much, "I never do anything I can't do from the back of a horse."

"Must be dif'cult, sometimes," he said. "I can think of a lot of things I couldn't do a-horseback."

When I offered no comment, we rode on in silence for some distance.

His horse was in poor shape. It had been hard-used for some time, but it had not been much of a horse to begin with. The man himself had a poor outfit, all except his rifle. That was in good shape, oiled and cared for. He had no hand gun anywhere that I could see, but I had learned not to be too trusting.

After a while he began to talk again, and his comments were prying ones. The less I said the more curious he became, so I finally said, "I like drifting. Never held to one job too long. I came out California way after a girl," which was at least partly true, "but

180

she took off with another man. Right now I'm just seeing country, but I'm trying to decide whether I should try to ride up Virginia City way, or turn back and ride north to Oregon. I've never been to either place."

"They ain't much. Anyways," he suggested, "a man would have to have eatin' money."

I chuckled. "Not if he rides the grub-line. I can always do a mite of work for a meal, if need be. I never paid much mind to money. I'm no hand for gambling, and as long as I can eat and sleep, I'll make out."

"Good horse you got there," he said. "Don't look like no cowhand's horse."

"Swapped for him," I lied. "I'd caught me a couple of wild ones, young stuff and pretty good. I swapped 'em for this one."

But my outfit was just a little too good for a cowhand to afford, and I felt that he believed none of it. The well-filled saddlebags continued to hold his attention. If given a chance, I was sure he would try to steal everything I had, and to murder me if chance allowed.

The miles fell behind us, and night drew near. The heat had gone, and here and there a star was appearing.

From time to time his horse started to lag behind, something to be expected considering the animal he rode, but I didn't like it, so I drew up and waited for him.

"Sorry, mister," he grumbled, "this here animal just

ain't able to keep up. You ride ahead and find a place to camp. We'll catch up."

"It's early to camp," I said.

There was something about him now that turned me cold inside, and I knew I didn't want to go to sleep in the same camp with him. I was dead-tired with the riding, the heat, and the dust, and I had relaxed from what I had gone through in the days just past. I knew I would sleep too soundly for my own safety. The way he eyed my horse and saddlebags left me only one conclusion, yet I could neither accuse him nor offer any good excuse for riding on without him.

My horse could easily outdistance his, but that would mean turning my back to him, something I certainly didn't want to do.

"Maybe you're right," I said after a moment. "I *am* tired."

Suddenly I saw a small cove in the hills with some clumps of brush. "There! That might be a good place."

He turned his head, and I drew my gun. When he turned back and started to speak he looked hard at me and then at the gun. He made no move at all. He was a very careful man.

"My friend," I said, "I don't know you. I like traveling alone, and so I'm going to leave you right here. Get off your horse."

He hesitated. For a moment I thought he was going to chance it, but he had no pistol in sight, and I could not figure him having anything larger than a derringer.

"You can't get away with this," he said, "leavin' a man afoot."

"You aren't going to be afoot," I said. "I'm just going to let you walk a mile to get your horse. I'll leave him tied up yonder."

"I done nothin' to you." His voice was surly.

"You had some ideas, though," I told him, "and I didn't care for them. I've got nothing anybody would want but this horse—"

"Yeah?" he sneered. But my gesture with the gun got him off the horse, and taking its bridle I rode away, keeping an eye on him nonetheless. A mile away I tied the horse to some brush, and lit out.

He could make that mile in fifteen minutes, I figured, but by that time I would be four or five miles off and still going.

The dun was ready for it. The horse had liked that man no more than I had, and felt like running in the cool air of evening.

It was wide-open country, gently rolling hills and little brush, and by day one could see for miles, but at night after a few yards a man was lost to view. I rode rapidly for perhaps three miles, then settled down to an easy lope and kept it up. The dun was a tough range-and-mountain horse, and was accustomed to going for long stretches.

From time to time I checked the Big Dipper for the time, watching it swing around the Pole Star. After a while I slowed the dun to a walk, but I kept on going. I should camp soon, but the thought of that old man on my trail worried me. He would be coming along, and he was not going to be easy to lose.

The country presently became more broken. Several times I deliberately turned off the trail to one side or the other, leaving well-defined tracks where I turned off, and returning to the trail in places where the tracks were not likely to be seen. But I had a hunch the old man was an Injun on the trail.

For five hours I rode, and then my own weariness and the growing weariness of my horse made me realize that I must turn off and find a camp. Taking a turn at a place in the deepest shadow of a rock, I scrambled up a steep trail and rode along the top of a mesa, then off the other edge into a deep canyon. Here there was a trail of sorts, for the dun kept going when I could see nothing but occasional glimpses of the whiter, hard-packed ground.

Of a sudden, I heard water. Rounding a corner of rock, I found myself in a small basin where a trickle of water fell into a pool. A few cottonwoods were there, and some willow brush, and it was as good a camping spot as a man could want. It was at least three-quarters of a mile off the trail, and in a spot where I'd be hard to find.

Picketing my horse on a small patch of grass, I unrolled my blankets on the far side of a cottonwood tree where the ground lay bare and smooth. With my saddle for a pillow, I was soon asleep, not forgetting to place my Colt close to my hand.

My eyes opened to broad daylight, and opened on

my strange pursuer. He sat his saddle not twenty feet away, and as I opened my eyes he shook out a loop. I started to come up fast, the loop shot out, and I had just warning enough to throw up an arm and get that as well as my neck, into the loop. Dropping my hand, I grasped the rope, but he slapped spurs to his horse and jumped him, and all that saved me was the sudden lunge I gave, throwing myself past the cottonwood tree and snubbing the rope there.

He brought up short, giving me a terrific jolt. I went to my knees, slammed into the tree, and he swung to ride around to get a loop around the tree, so as to bind me there. My hand grabbed at my blankets and came up with my Colt.

Too late he saw the gun, and grabbed at his chest. I fired, holding the gun in my left hand, and scored a clean miss on him, but burned his horse across the shoulder.

The crow-bait gave a startled leap, throwing his aim off target, and I got off a second shot and missed again. The rope had slacked briefly and I threw it off, flattening myself behind the cottonwood. I heard his gun roar and heard the bullet thud into the tree, but my pistol was in my right hand now and I jumped into the clear.

He had a big Colt in his hand. "Got you!" he yelled, and threw the gun up to chop down, as some men will do.

I shot, not looking at the gun, but only at him. My bullet caught him in the side above the hip, but he managed to fire. It was too close a miss for comfort, and I jumped back past the cottonwood. As my feet hit ground on the other side of the tree, I shot again. He reeled in the saddle, gave me a glaring look, and slapping spurs to the crow-bait, was away at a dead run.

For a moment I could only stand and stare after him. He was hit twice, one of them a good one, at least, but that was a tough old man. I wanted to see no more of him, ever.

The dun seemed undisturbed, by which I gathered he had been around gunfire before. Saddling up, I gathered my gear and rode out of there on the far side of the hollow, wary of every possible place of ambush.

Only then did I realize that my knees were badly torn from being jerked along the gravel and into the tree, my arm had a rope-burn that began to sting as sweat got into it. I also was developing a stiff neck, and a rope burn on it as well.

"That was a mean old man," I said, speaking to the dun, who flicked an ear at me.

Talking to a horse was not a new thing for me, or for any man who rides miles over lonely country. But then, I always figured horses were as good as people, or better, and I took them into my confidence from time to time. That line-back dun was a good listener, and had to be, for I'd had the scare of my life and was talking it out of my system.

Of course, that old man figured he just had a wet-eared kid, but I'd gotten some lead into his system that was going to take some digesting. Nevertheless, I scouted the country carefully as I rode, and kept on riding the day through.

When I finally got to Walker's Pass, two men were camped there with some sheep.

In answer to my question one of them said, "Three days ago—Bob Heseltine and two others and a woman. They went through the pass and I figure they're headed north from there.

"You know Heseltine?" I asked. They asked me to eat with them, and I joined them.

"Seen him kill a man in a saloon down Texas way. That was seven, eight years ago. He shot that man down with no reason at all but that he didn't like him."

He looked at me. "Are you Shell Tucker?"

"Yes."

"Heard you was huntin' him. Good luck."

"There may be a man hunting me," I told them, finishing my coffee. Then, as they were hungry for news, or for any sort of diversion, I told them about my encounter with the old man.

They listened, exchanging looks. "That old man, now—he about five-seven or -eight? Weigh about a hundred and forty? With a kind of white scar near his mouth?"

"You know him?"

"Boy, you tackled an ol' he-coon. That there was Pony Zale. He's a claim-jumper, a hoss thief, and more than once a murderer, but nobody ain't never proved it on him.

"Down Ruidoso way he come up with some Mexicans drivin' sheep, and offered to help. Of a sudden, a couple of days later, he cut loose with his Winchester and killed two of them. The third man came runnin' back to camp, and he shot him . . . on'y that man didn't die. He lived to tell of it.

"A posse set out, but he'd sold the sheep and left the country. He's a bad one."

"Well, I got lead into him," I said, "but he was still in the saddle when he left out of there, and he didn't look too happy about the way things turned out."

One of the men chuckled. "If he shows up, you went south."

The coffee had been good, the beans better, and I hated to ride on, but time was against me and Bob Heseltine was riding away.

Down the trail a piece, I looked back. The trail was empty, but I had an uneasy feeling that the hunter had become the hunted.

CHAPTER 17

There's nothing like time alone to give a man a chance to check up on himself, and I expect it was high time that I stopped to look at my hole card.

A lot of miles had been left in the dust behind me, and I'd been in a few shootups, and here I was no nearer to what I'd set out to do. And all the while, back there in Colorado was Vashti. And the more I thought of Vashti, the more I thought what a fool I was to go traipsing off across the country. By now she might even be married.

Married?

That pulled me up short, and the dun, too. Just the thought of it gave me a twinge, but why not? I'd staked no claim on that girl.

There was no reason at all why she should wait, but the thought of her marrying some no-account . . .

Of course, that was a cause for thinking, too, because a man has to be honest with himself. What did I mean . . . no-account? Mightn't folks say that of me?

I had nothing. No claim, no shack, just a two-bit layout down Texas way that by now was probably occupied by somebody else. I had no means to make a living beyond punching cows or doing day labor, and that surely wasn't enough for Vashti . . . even if she might think it was.

Somewhere along there I lost all track of Bob Heseltine and them.

From time to time there'd been tracks of a sort, and I'd been sure in my mind I was on the trail. That old dun was nobody's fool, and he knew I was trailing somebody. I think that dun even put me back on the trail a couple of times.

Where could they go but straight ahead? If I knew Ruby Shaw, she wouldn't cotton to any hide-out camp in the Sierras, which reared up on my left, nor would she take to Death Valley, which lay yonder beyond the Panamints. She would want to head for Virginia City, where they were taking silver out of the Comstock.

Come to think of it, these men must be catching billy-hell right now, Heseltine and the others. Almost ever since they got that money, months ago now, they'd been riding. She hadn't had much chance to pleasure herself with having money, and she wasn't the kind to let it lay. She would be nagging at those boys to do something about me.

Moreover, this was a pretty good place in which to do whatever they had a mind to. The mountains and the desert left few trails open for travel, and even after Death Valley was past there was still a lot of wide-open dry country to the east.

Suddenly, I found their tracks again. Four riders, and not very far ahead of me, by the look of them.

A man doesn't travel as far as I had without learning something, and I'd been trailing tough, dangerous men. I'd had brief showdowns with both Sites and Reese, but so far I'd never actually locked horns with Heseltine. But now they were together again . . . or so it appeared.

Yet I wondered about Doc. His share of the money had probably been mentally divided among them, but now he had returned, and would be making claims.

Well, the element that makes a man a thief makes him untrustworthy, but those who associate with him often forget that. Doc Sites was neither needed or wanted, least of all by Ruby Shaw.

I'd not done much but just hang on, nagging at their heels, watching for my chance. Everywhere I went the story was there ahead of me, like at the sheep camp, where those men had known who I was.

And likely the outlaws, their ears to the ground, heard the stories, too.

The Owens River valley where I now rode was all of a hundred miles long and five to twelve miles wide. On the west were the Sierras, a rugged range that seemed to rise abruptly from the valley floor. On the other side the Inyo-White ranges rose in places to over 11,000 feet.

Both ranges were alive with game, and in some areas were alive with Indians. Neither was a place to spend money or enjoy the fleshpots of Egypt, so I had no idea the outlaws would stay in that area.

The valley looked to me like a great fault-block that had sunk. I'd picked up a smattering of geology from Con Judy during our rides, and had begun looking at deserts and mountains from fresh viewpoints, and it showed me that the more a man knew, the more interesting everything became. As Con had said, if you didn't have books to read, you could always read the face of nature.

All around me were signs of change in the earth. Decomposing rock trickled down from notches in the hills, spreading wider and wider as they reached the valley floor, like great fans spread out. And in some areas heat and cold, thawing and freezing were helping the roots of trees to break up the soil, even to break up rocks.

Going ahead rapidly was out of the question here, for there were too many possibilities of ambush. Carefully not following any pattern, I varied my route from time to time, leaving the trail to the right or left, following the slope of one mountain or the other, suddenly changing direction, and using every bit of cover that I could. I knew they were somewhere ahead of me, and judging by an occasional track, they were only hours ahead.

And I watched my back trail. How badly Pony Zale had been wounded I did not know, but I had a feeling that tough old man would want some of his own back. He would be hunting me as I hunted them.

Con Judy's talk of rocks and rock formations, as well as the possibility that some plants indicated minerals in the earth beneath them, kept my eyes on the country even as much as fear of ambush. I was well up the mountainside, riding through a scattering of trees and stopping from time to time to study the terrain ahead and in the valley, when my eyes were drawn to a smooth surface of rock, which must have been polished by a glacier. Here and there were places where weathering had broken the surface into pits, or wider areas that looked like great sores eating at the smooth face. Suddenly my eye caught a place where the surface had been broken . . . and recently.

Drawing rein in the shelter of some pines, I studied the spot. A horse's hoof had broken that edge, and left in the place where it had broken off, a clear print of half a shoe.

Somebody had gone up that slope not long ago, just ahead of me.

That somebody was up there now. Had they seen me coming? Had they seen me draw up?

My mouth was dry, and all at once I was wary. I slid from the saddle, Winchester in hand. Moving quickly, I tied my horse to a clump of brush, then crouching low, I moved up among the rocks.

Beyond this area were scattered, stunted pines and a few cedars. Among the trees, and beyond them, the surface was broken.

The sun was behind the wall of the Sierras, but it still held a golden rim on top of the White Mountains opposite. Shadows were growing where I waited, and the silence of evening was over the land. Somewhere a dove called, another answered.

Easing my crouching position, I continued to wait. My spot was fairly good, hidden from the higher slope by rocks and trees, exposed to the valley below, but a valley that lay empty, so far as I could see. What I must be wary of was before or behind me.

Suddenly, somewhere on the slope ahead I heard two racketing shots, and then the slowly dying echo of them fading away among the canyons and along the mountainside. Those shots must have been fired a good four or five hundred yards off, and no bullet came close to me. I waited, listening.

For a long time there was no sound, and then a faint rattle of rocks came from somewhere up ahead, and a flicker of movement, followed by silence. The shadows grew longer as I waited. Returning to my horse, I untied it and stepped into the saddle.

I rode ahead warily, keeping to the shadows and trying for areas of grass or leaf mold where the hoofs of my horse would make no sound.

Who had fired? And at whom?

All at once, just as we started between two close-growing pines, the dun shied violently. Gun in hand, I held him still, listening.

No sound . . . only the wind in the pines.

Peering ahead in the gathering gloom, my eyes caught the shape of something lying on the ground. I stepped down from my horse, waited a moment, then moved forward on cat feet.

It was a man, lying on his face, and he was dead. I did not need an examination to know that. He had been shot twice in the back, at close range.

Even before I turned the body over, I knew who it was. Doc Sites should never have followed Reese and Heseltine to California. He had come up here with them, or had been followed, and then been executed . . . murdered.

He was never much of a man, I thought, although at one time he had seemed smart and almost glamorous to me. He had always been a tin-horn, living from stealing cattle or horses, and given to too much talk. But now I felt sorry for the man. Nobody should die like that, murdered by those he had believed to be his friends, left unburied on the lonely mountain for the buzzards and the coyotes.

There was nothing I could do but roll him into a hollow among the rocks, and pile rocks and brush over the body. His pockets had been emptied. His horse and guns were gone.

Angling down the slope, I found a vague trail along the mountainside and followed it.

When I had gone no more than two miles the trail turned suddenly up the slope, and I went along it. From time to time I dismounted to crouch low and study the trail. There were no tracks.

Those who had murdered Sites had gone on down to the main trail on the valley floor. The one I followed was an Indian trail, and it suddenly reached a small hollow under a rocky overhang where there was a pool of water fed by a trickle from out of the rocks. It was a sheltered, hidden spot, with grass for the dun, and a good quiet place for me.

Over a tiny fire I made coffee and soup from dried peas and jerked beef. I was tired, and it tasted good.

For a long time I lay awake, looking up through the leaves of a pin oak at the stars above. I listened to the stirrings of the night, and heard nothing that warned of danger. But I thought of Vashti, and found myself wanting again to be back in Colorado.

It came over me suddenly that I must end the chase. I must quit and find a place for myself, some-thing beyond this endless pursuit, or I would someday end as Doc Sites had, shot in the back . . . murdered.

I went to sleep then, sure that I had arranged my future. And taking no thought for what destiny might have in store. A man may plan, but there are movements beyond his plannings, there are events born of powers that lie beyond him.

As always, unless very tired, I woke up just before daylight. For a few minutes I lay still, getting the feel of the morning. It was clear but still dark, only a few bright stars remaining in the sky.

A cool wind was just barely stirring the leaves. The dun was munching contentedly at some brush he had found near the camp.

After a moment I threw off my blankets, decided on what I would do.

I tugged on my boots, rolled my blankets, and saddled up, warming the bit for a few minutes inside my shirt, for the morning was chilly. Once saddled and ready, I tied the dun to a shrub and, taking my Winchester, went up through the trees to an outcropping I'd seen the night before. Beside it, where my body would not be outlined, I studied the terrain below.

There were the usual stirrings of birds and animals. A few doves talked in the brush. From a tree some distance off a mockingbird sang. Wherever I looked, there was no sign of a fire, and on the trail below, which I could make out as a dim gray streak, nothing moved.

My chase was over—that was the decision I'd come to the night before, and the one my morning thoughts agreed with. It was no way for a man to spend his life.

Now, not seeing me would worry Heseltine and his friends more than seeing me. They would not believe that I had dropped the pursuit, and would feel they must grow increasingly wary, not knowing when I might again appear.

Over a small fire I made coffee, fried bacon, and ate the last of the sourdough bread I'd been saving. Once more I checked the trail . . . nothing there.

Mounting up, I went down the trail on an angle, deliberately crossed it, and rode into the White Mountains with my mind made up.

I'd cross over into Nevada, strike the stage route that led through Eureka, and on to Salt Lake, and then I'd ride back to Colorado.

These were barren, lonely mountains . . . at least along the trail I was riding, and after a few miles the silence began to wear on my nerves. For there was no sound except what my horse made, my spurs jingling, or the creak of my saddle. Several times I drew up, listening, feeling suspicious of the morning.

The sun was bright, the day unbelievably clear. The sky was a calm blue, with only thin, very high clouds, so flimsy as scarcely to be seen.

The dim trail wound higher and higher, but allowed me no view of itself for more than a few hundred yards at any time. The dun was nervous, his ears twitching at every sound, but finally we topped out on a bald knob of the mountain, with a tremendous view to the east of a wide, barren land, sometimes showing the bared teeth of outcroppings, or scattered juniper, and here and there the white splotches of dried alkali lakes. Nowhere did I see any indication of water.

At noon, in the shade of a juniper larger than usual, I stopped to rest my horse. The area was wide open and empty, as free of cover as a bald head. Having picketed the dun, I stretched out in the shade of the tree.

Overhead the sky was wide and empty. Before I closed my eyes, I looked around carefully, and there was nothing, simply nothing at all. My eyes closed, and I slept.

The warmth of the sun, the clearness of the air, and my own weariness were enough, and my sleep was sound. After all, I was alone in this empty land.

Through the haze of sleep, something grated, there was a faint stirring, something tugged at my waist, and I opened my eyes looking into the muzzle of my own six-shooter.

Pony Zale was seated on his haunches not ten feet away. His grinning lips showed broken teeth, but there was no smile in his cold eyes. "Got you this time," he said.

Slowly, I sat up. "Figured you were dead," I lied. "I got lead into you, didn't I?"

"You surely did." He spat a brown stream close to my boot. "I'm still packin' some of it, but it takes a lot to put me down. Bullet was never made to kill me. Old fortune tellin' woman, a gypsy woman, she told me that, so I never worry."

His horse was nearby, right alongside my dun. My saddlebags were on his horse now, only his horse was no longer the crow-bait.

"You've got you a new horse," I commented.

"Yes, sir. I got me a good one. Better'n your dun, I'm thinkin'. The man wouldn't have been wishful to give it up, so I taken no chances. I surely do hate to be refused."

He spat again. "You know what you got comin', don't you?"

I grinned at him. "Why, sure! You and me are going to ride down to Carson City and have us a drink at one of those fancy drinkin' places where the politicians go. I'll even stand treat . . . that is, I will if you've left me any money."

"Well, now, that there's a thought. I might even take you up on it if n you hadn't put lead into me. I don't take to that at all."

He was on his feet in one easy, fluid movement, unexpected in a man of his years. "No, sir. I don't take to gettin' shot at, nor hit. I'm a-goin' to kill you. I ain't a-goin' to kill you outright just put lead into you and ride off an let you die.

"This here trail you've chose ain't been used in a couple hundred years or more. The Pah-Utes say it's a medicine trail, and they won't ride it. No white man knows of it . . . except me.

"There ain't no water in fifty mile, and I don't figure you're going to make that much with a bullet in you. Not with you losin' blood, and no water."

"You'd better kill me, Pony," I said casually, "because I'll track you down and have your hide for this."

He chuckled. "You're game. Game as hell, but 't won't do you no good."

There wasn't one chance in a million, but I came off the ground in a long dive. I heard the bellow of his gun, felt a brutal slam alongside my skull, and went down into the gravel.

The gun bellowed again, and I felt my body twitch as it took the second bullet.

"Well, now," I heard him say. "Reckon that'll hold you. If'n you catch up to me now, you'll surely earn what you get."

There was a sound of a horse's hoofs retreating, and then a vast emptiness. And then, for the first time, I felt the pain. The pain, and the hot, hot sun.

CHAPTER 18

It was dark . . . dark and cold. My head throbbed horribly, and my mouth was dry. I lay very still against the earth, only I was no longer up on the mountain. Somehow, some way, I had gotten myself into a ravine.

The canyon walls sloped back steeply on either side, but I had no idea where I was, or how I had got there. Yet under me was the trail. I could feel it with my hands. Covered with dirt as I found myself to be, I thought, I must have rolled down the side of the canyon and landed in the trail.

I grasped rocks at the side and pulled myself along.

There was no conscious thought of trying to survive, only that terrible drive to keep moving, not to stop. It was in my mind that I must get somewhere, and I must be there soon.

Somewhere along the line I must have ceased to be conscious, or at least, to have any sense of awareness. For when I realized anything at all, it was the warmth of the sun, and I was no longer in a ravine, but in a sandy wash in an open area—a *playa,* as the Spanish call a dry lake.

A shadow passed over me, momentary, fleeting. After a moment, it passed again . . . or perhaps it was another shadow.

I turned my head, looking up and around. It was a buzzard. It was several buzzards.

Somebody had told me they went for the kidneys first. It was a man I had met who had fought in China. He said the vultures always tried for the kidneys, not always waiting until a man was dead. If you went down, he said, always pull something over your kidneys, some protection.

My holster was empty, but he had not taken my knife—maybe because I was waking up. In all the crawling and rolling it had stayed in its scabbard, with the rawhide thong to hold it there. Slipping the thong, I got it out.

"Come on!" I yelled. "Come on down here!"

They did not come.

They were old at this game. Buzzards have patience built into them, a patience born of the knowledge that all things die, and they have only to wait.

Knife back in the scabbard again, thong in place, I crawled on because there was nothing else to do. My body was sore, my head was a huge hollow drum in which something pounded. My mouth was full of cotton and I could not feel my tongue. All through the endless heat, I crawled and crawled.

My hands grew bloody, the flesh was raw, and the blood left traces on the trail, but still I crawled.

How far I went each time I had no idea. Ahead of me I would see a stone and would drag myself as far as that stone. When I reached it after a long time, I chose another stone, and dragged myself to that one.

I was realizing now that the second bullet had hit me in the side, and the place was awfully sore. There was no doubt about where the first bullet had hit, because the throbbing in my head told me. There might be a hole in it, but I did not want to know.

Another rock ahead, and I crawled on. Then a juniper tree. I crawled . . . and then I passed out. I awakened in the dark, and this time I crawled toward a low star somewhere ahead of me. It was a reddish star . . . Mars, maybe. I'd heard that Mars was a red planet.

But crawling on, I somehow got too close to a bank and rolled over, hit bottom, or seemed to; a rock gave way and I fell straight down, landing with a thud. Pain shot through my skull and I passed out once again.

The sun was hot when I tried to open my eyes. My lids were thick and heavy. There was nothing in my mouth but a dry stick where my tongue should be.

I was lying in the bottom of a narrow gulch. Looking up, I could see where I had fallen . . . all of six feet. Above there was the sunlight and the sky, the lovely clear blue sky. I rolled over on my belly and looked down the gulch. Rocks, water-worn and smooth, small rocks, huge boulders, with two banks rising high above me.

Vashti . . . I was going back to Vashti. I had started out to go there, and she would be waiting. I crawled again, and something hammered inside my skull, waves of heat and cold swept over me. My hands were ugly to look at, the blood was stiff with sand and gravel and gray dust.

No longer did I sense clearly whether it was night or day. Dimly I chose rocks, junipers, anything to crawl to. I chewed on leaves. I tore at a prickly pear, ripping my bloody hands on its thorns, but crushing some of the pulp into my mouth. It was sticky, but wet.

And again in the heat there were those shadows that passed over me. I finally crawled into a hollow under a rock and lay there for some minutes with my eyes closed.

The sand was damp, and with my bloody hands, I dug into it until soaking blobs of sand came up, and I lay in the wet sand drinking in the coolness through my dry, parched skin. Water was around my hand. My hand was in water.

It was slowly seeping in, it was muddy, but it was water.

I lowered my sore face into it, drank a little, then drew back away from it. After a while I drank again. I bathed my face with it, bathed the blood from my raw hands. I put water on my neck, my face. Then I dipped my head into it to my eyebrows and held it there. After a moment I lay back again.

My pants were torn, but I found where the bullet had gone in right under the belt. Moving the belt, I bathed the wound. It looked inflamed and ugly.

I felt that the sun would kill me if I went out in it again. I must wait until night. I stayed in the hollow, poured water over me, waited for it to seep in once more, and then drank again. After that I slept, and it was dark when I woke up. I took a long drink, then got to my feet.

Outside of the hollow where I stood, I could make out the trail, still slanting away from me. I found a stick nearby, and took it for a staff. Then I started to walk, hobbling a little because my side was painful.

I was going to live. I was going back to Vashti. I was going back to her, but first I was going to find Pony.

Most of the night I walked, with occasional rests, and toward dawn I hunted for shelter. With the first rays of the sun I found three junipers bunched together and I crawled into their partial shade. By hunching myself up and moving a bit as the sun moved, I stayed in shade the long day through.

Then I started on, walking, falling sometimes, but moving along. Far ahead of me I saw a star, a star low down—too low.

A campfire . . . I broke into a stumbling run, but fell

after only a few steps, exhausted.

After a while I got to my feet. The fire was still there, but dimmer now. I struggled on, walking, falling, crawling, then getting up to walk again.

After a long time the fire was nearer. Day was coming. When day came the man whose camp that was would mount and ride away, and then I would be lost. There could be no town within miles, or even a ranch or a settlement. I had to make it.

I tried to break into a run again, but I couldn't manage it. But I was getting closer, and now I could see a thin blue trail of smoke rising.

It was there. There was a fire, and there was some-body at the fire!

I tried to yell, but no sound came. I went ahead . . . and then I was at the fire.

Two horses . . . *Pony.*

He got up, staring in horror at me. Then he let out a hoarse scream and grabbed at his rifle. I lunged at him, but I fell, and heard the bellow of his gun.

I heard it again, felt the sting of sand kicked into my face, and then I got up, and I swung my stick. He lifted a hand to catch it, and as he did I dived at him.

He tried to step back, but tripped and went down. He got up, but I swung at his face, my fist smashing his nose. He fell back into the fire, but rolled clear, grab-bing for a gun. I swung a burning stick at his face and when his hand came up to ward it off, the flame enveloped his hand. He gave a scream and staggered back, then swung at my head with a stick. The blow caught me across the forehead and I went down, twisting as I went, to fall clear of the fire.

Again I was struggling back to consciousness, again it was night.

The fire was still smoking a little, but no flame showed. Pony was gone, the horses were gone. His frying pan was there, and his coffeepot. He must have jumped into the saddle and fled.

I got to my knees, reached the coffeepot. Coffee sloshed in it and I drank. It was very hot, but I hardly noticed. After a moment I put the coffeepot down and poked at the fire, found some unburned ends and added them to it. I tried to blow, but my lips were broken and bloody, and I almost cried out with the pain as they cracked open again.

But a flame sprang up. I looked in the frying pan. Shriveled pieces of bacon lay there, and I ate them. Turning my neck stiffly, I looked around. Evidently Pony had been packed to go when I appeared, and had simply leaped into the saddle after he struck me down.

I drank more of the coffee, and felt better, but I hated the look of my hands. The cracks had opened and they were bleeding again.

My knife was still there, and my stick was there, too.

Nothing seemed right. How had I come up to him when he was riding horseback and I was afoot? Why was he not far out of the country?

Again I drank coffee, but when there was still some left I put it back close to the fire. I added fuel, and lay down on the cold ground.

Vashti . . .

Dawn came cold and gloomy. Shivering, I drank the last of the coffee, scraped the fire apart so it would die quickly on the bare ground, and then I started.

My legs were stiff, and I hobbled, but I moved.

When I had gone only a short distance I fell, and this time I did not get up. One leg drew up, but it slipped back, and I lay still.

I was not unconscious, nor was I quite conscious. I was vaguely aware that it had started to sprinkle.

Rain.

Feebly, I struggled to turn over, trying to get on my back.

Somebody was watching me. The thought slowly seeped into my dulled brain. *Somebody was watching me!*

It could not be. I was going crazy. I managed to roll on my back and opened my mouth. Slowly the rain fell over me, some water trickled down my throat, and my face felt good. My body was chilled and stiff, but somehow refreshed.

My head lifted, I looked around, fell back. *Somebody was watching me.*

They were Indians. There were forty or fifty of them and there were no women or children among them. They were painted for war, and every man was armed.

I rolled over slowly, got my hands under me, and stood up. Some Utes, traveling back from a fight with the Comanches had once stayed at our ranch, recovering from their wounds. Pa had let them have three horses, although we were hard-up. But while they were there I had learned a little of their language. These would be Pah-utes. I spoke to them.

They looked at me. I tried English. "Much hurt," I said. "Bad man shoot me. I have no gun. I follow. He run."

"You follow Medicine Trail."

The Indian who spoke was weirdly gotten up. A medicine man?

"Yes. The Sky Chief tells me to follow the Medicine Road and the Pah-ute will help me."

They stared at me, muttering among themselves. It was different from the tongue I knew, but it was similar. Sometimes only a word or two seemed right; sometimes a whole sentence fell into place for me.

They led several spare horses, and suddenly a slim warrior rode over to me with a horse, and catching hold on the mane, I swung to its back.

They led off swiftly, and clinging to the mane, I rode with them.

Their village was miles away, but somehow I clung to the horse and kept on with them. When we came to the village at last, I saw that it was made up of perhaps two dozen lodges huddled in a cluster on a bench above a ravine. The position was good—it was sheltered, and there was water and fuel.

For four days I lay in their village and they fed and cared for me. An old woman came into the lodge where I was and took care of my wounds.

On the fifth day I walked out of the lodge. I was weak, but felt I was able to go.

"What you do now?" the chief asked.

"I will go to the white man's town and find the man who shot me."

"You have no gun."

"I will find a gun."

"You have no horse."

"I ask my red brother to lend me one. I will return it if I am able, or I will pay you."

"My people are at war with your people."

"I did not know this. I have been where the Great Water lies, under the setting sun. I go back where my squaw is, in Colorado."

He smoked and thought. Then he said, "You brave man. We follow your blood . . . many miles. You find your enemy, you kill." He looked up at me. "I have no gun to give, but I will give pony."

He pointed with his pipe. "You take that one."

It was a mouse-colored horse, about fourteen hands, a good horse.

"Thank you." I walked over to the horse, which was fitted with a hackamore.

Swinging astride, I rode up to his fire. "You are a great chief," I said, "and you are my friend. If any man asks you, say you are a friend of Shell Tucker."

Turning, I rode away, and they stood together, watching me go.

I looked back once. They were a war party, and I had seen fresh scalps.

CHAPTER 19

Within the hour I had picked up the trail. Two horses, one led. And I knew the tracks of that line-back dun as I knew the cracks in my own hands.

The grulla I rode was a good horse. The Pah-ute had given me a good one because he knew I had a long chase ahead of me, and he knew what sort of horse a man needed when the trail stretched on for uncounted miles. Its gait was smooth. That horse was no show-boat, but he'd get in there and stay until the sun was gone and the moon was up.

When I came down out of those bleak, bitter mountains with the taste of alkali on my lips and my skin white from the dust of it, I had no idea where I was, only that I was riding east.

First it had been Bob Heseltine and Kid Reese. Now it was Zale. I'd find him somewhere up ahead, or he'd find me, and that would be an end to all of it, or part of it, depending on who saw who first.

A rugged, rawboned range lay before me, and across the flat of a vanished lake the jagged peaks lifted up. Not high . . . not many of those desert ranges are high, but they are dry, and they are all jagged edge, broken rock, and plants with thorns ready to tear the flesh.

A trail showed . . . a trail that had seen some use, though not lately—except for that lone-riding man with two horses.

The trail pointed into the saw-toothed ridges, and I pointed the grulla that way and said, "Their way is our way, boy. Let's be a-goin'."

I thought of Con Judy, who was my friend, and I thought of Vashti, who might be waiting or might not, and I thought of all the brutal, battered, and savage land that lay between us, and me without even a gun.

If he waited for me somewhere up in those rocks, he'd have me. If he waited I was dead meat . . . buzzard and coyote meat. But I had an idea he was running hard, and I stayed on the trail.

We climbed . . . higher and higher.

Suddenly a rider showed. A lone man riding a mule, leading another with a pack. A prospector.

He drew up when he saw me, not liking it. And there was a reason why, for my face was blistered and broken, my hands were only half-healed, my clothes were torn, and a sight.

"Howdy," he said. "Mister, wherever you been I don't wanna go.

"I'm comin' out," I said. "I made it. There's Indians back yonder though, and they're wearing their paint."

"I seen 'em before," he said. "I cut my teeth on Injuns."

"You got a gun to spare? I need a gun."

"Boy, by the look of you you need a bed for two weeks, and a bath every day of it. You're riding death, boy. You should look at you from this side of your eyes."

"I need a gun. You passed a man up yonder with two horses, and my guns as well as his own. At least, I believe he's got them. You loan me a gun and I'll send you twice the cost of it, wherever you are."

"I seen that man, boy, and you stay shut of him. That's a mean man, too much for a boy like you. I seen him this time because I seen him a-comin', and I knew who he was by the way he sets his horse. I cut out of the trail and when he seen my tracks he looked up to where I was, bedded down in the rocks, and I told him, 'Pony, you keep right on a-ridin'. I got you dead in my sights.' He kept on, and you know something? That wasn't like him. It wasn't like him a-tall."

"He's riding scared," I said.

"I ain't got a gun to spare, and if I had it I wouldn't lend it to a man who's going to get himself killed. What's your name, boy?"

"Shell Tucker," I said, "and I've followed some trails before this. . . . Be seeing you."

The grulla clung to the trail like a hound dog. He was all I'd figured he was. He clung to that trail as if it was him Pony had tried to kill. We made our night camp at Cave Springs.

The Pah-utes had given me a double handful of jerky and I chewed a piece for supper, and drank at the spring. I'd moved back from the spring among some rocks when I heard a horse coming.

It was a long, lean cowhand riding a sorrel gelding, and he drew up at the spring and started to get down, and then he saw my tracks. He started to swing his horse, and I said, "Don't be in such an all-fired hurry. I don't even have a gun."

"Then stand quiet," he said, "because I do have. You just stand easy until I look you over." He sidled his horse around until he could get a good look at me. "You don't look fit to do no harm," he said. "What happened to you?"

"You'd better ask that of a man you sighted down yonder with a led horse. Have you got a spare gun you could lend me? Anything that can shoot."

"No. I got only this six-shooter and my Winchester, and where I'm going I'm likely to need them both. What happened?" he asked again.

"Have you got some coffee? I have nothing but beef jerky some Indians gave me."

"I've got it, and I was just fixin' to make it up," he said. He got down very careful, and kept his horse between us until he could see I really was unarmed. Then he holstered his gun and stripped his gear from the horse.

"Good water?" he asked.

"Any water is good. If you don't think it is, try going where I've been without it."

We got us a fire going and he put coffee on and broke open a can of beans, giving me half and keeping the other half for himself. And while the coffee boiled I told him what had happened since I'd seen that mean old man on the trail.

"He's down there in Silver Peak," he said. "These here are the Silver Peak Mountains, and the town is down yonder on the edge of Clayton Valley."

"Is it much of a town?"

"Not so's you could notice. She was fetching up to be and then the color ran out, and the folks just left. There's a store or two, there's a place where you can sleep inside out of the rain, and there's a corral for your horse.

"And there's a stamp mill that ain't running no more, and a lot of folks setting around saying how there's millions just under the ground. There may be, but I don't know of what. It surely ain't cash money. You ride in there and flash a five-dollar bill and they're likely to give you the place and run."

"I couldn't flash a five-cent piece," I said. "That man cleaned me."

"Well, I got two bucks, mister, and I'll split her right down the middle with you. I ain't going to see any pilgrim ride into that town broke."

"How about a gun?"

"Uh-uh. You get killed on your own time, with your own gun."

"If I can't find a gun I'll cut myself a stick," I told him. "I want some hide off that man."

The beans were good, the coffee better, and he divided a chunk of sourdough betwixt us. He was a good man, and he never told me his name, even. At the end, I did give him mine.

"If you ever come to Colorado," I said, "look me up. I'm Shell Tucker."

"Heard of you," he said. "They're beginning to

make up songs about you."

Silver Peak was a town not much more than ten, twelve years old and it was dead already . . . but nobody believed it, and when you've got that kind of faith, who's to say?

At the saloon three men were sitting on the porch under the overhang, and they watched me ride in. I kept a sharp lookout, but saw no sign of Pony or his horses. I rode up to the saloon and stepped down.

"I'm looking for a man with two horses," I said, "and the right to own only one of them."

"He's gone. And if you take my advice you'll forget him. He didn't look to me like he wanted to be found."

"I need a little grub and a gun," I told them.

"Mister, this here town is broke. Nobody has anything but what he needs. You ride right along."

"I got a dollar," I said.

"That'll buy you a mite of something. You ride on, boy. We got us a marshal here who don't cotton to man-hunting."

"Where is he?"

They pointed out a shack to me and I got back on my horse and rode over there. I got down in front of the shanty and went up the walk.

The man who opened the door was tall, lean, and hard-featured, and he wore a gun as if he knew what it was for. Behind him a woman was putting grub on the table.

"I'm Shell Tucker," I said, "and I'm hunting a man. I need a gun and a grubstake."

"Come in." He turned his head. "Ma, set up another place. This feller looks like he could use it."

When I sat down at the table the man tipped back in his chair, lit his pipe, and looked me over. "I'm Dean Blaisdell, and I am not long in Silver Peak. This here's a thankless job that pays enough to keep body and soul together. Now tell me about it."

So I told the story again, and by this time I'd streamlined it some. He needed only to look at me to see what I'd been through.

"Can't figure them redskins. Lucky they didn't take your hair."

"They'd followed me quite a spell. I guess they thought the country had made me suffer enough."

"Give you a horse, too? That's prime. I never knew that to happen, although they always cotton to a man who can take it.

"Tell you what I'll do. I taken a six-shooter off a man here a couple of months ago. It's a fine weapon. I'll let you have it, and ma and me will fix you a bait of grub.

"You'll need a saddle for that grulla, and there's one over to the livery stable. The owner pulled out and he just left it . . . where he was going he said he hoped never to see another."

We talked of places and people. He was an Arkansawyer, who had lived three years in Texas, had come on west and married the widow of a man killed by the Apaches in Arizona. They had followed one boom after another. "We made a little, but only to tide us over. I was a marshal in Ehrenburg for a few weeks, so they gave me this job."

His wife poured more coffee. "Heard about you an' Heseltine," Blaisdell said. "I seen him once . . . a dangerous man, I'd say,. but he was quiet when he was around my neck of the woods and gave no trouble to anybody.

"Lucky," he added, "I'd never want to tangle horns with a man like him. I pack a gun and I do my job, but I've never drawn a gun on a man in my life, and never saw a gunfight."

"I have," his wife said, "and I'd as soon never see another."

"Ma growed up in Injun country," Blaisdell explained.

"Never found no good in them," she said brusquely, "although I've known folks who lived among 'em. Their ways simply ain't Christian."

"I guess they were reared without any of that teaching," I suggested. "You've got to think of that. Their beliefs are different from ours."

"They surely are. But the gunfight I saw wasn't between white men and Indians. It was just some drunken cowboys in the street . . . at least folks said they was drunk. One of them was a gun-fanner and he done scattered lead all over the neighborhood. I say if men are going to shoot at each other they should shoot straight."

"That's the general idea, ma'am," I said.

"Are you going to kill that Bob Heseltine when you

find him? Like the stories say?"

"I don't want to kill anybody. I just want my money back."

"He's likely spent it," she said. "Money burns a hole in a man's pocket."

My dollar was still in my pocket when I rode through Paymaster Canyon into Big Smoky Valley. I'd pulled my stakes from Silver Peak before the sun was in the sky, and by the time I was well out into Big Smoky the sun was setting beyond the Monte Cristo Mountains, so red with their own color as well as the sun that they looked like flames against the sky.

Time and again I turned in my saddle to look back at them. They had a rare beauty, and when the shadows began to creep out from them their ridges were still crested with fire.

Nighttime found me at Montezuma's Well, with the stars bright overhead. There was a patch of grass there, and a few head of somebody's cows, and I settled down for the night. The tracks of the two horses were pointing north toward the mountains that loomed up, miles away.

My hands worried me. They were healing, but not fast enough, and I had no rifle. Crossing this bald plain I could be seen for miles, and Pony was too wise an old mountain and desert man not to check his back trail. "Boy," I said to myself, "when you reach those mountains you better ride loose in the saddle. He'll surely be staked out and waiting."

Next morning I was well started before the sun

chinned itself on the San Antonios. When I was nooning in the sandy wash where the Peavine seemed to peter out I was at a place where the trails divided. One went northwest toward the Toiyabe Mountains, and it was unmarked by man or beast. The other followed the Big Smoky Valley, and it was covered with tracks. Somebody—four or five or more men—had herded a bunch of cattle up that trail, and only their tracks remained.

Logically, as there were no tracks on the northwest trail, Zale must have taken the northeast branch up the valley, but I didn't believe it.

If I was running and a tracker was following, what would I do? I'd loose my tracks with that herd of cattle coming along behind, and when I was well along I'd find some hard surface and cut over where I'd leave no tracks to the other trail.

How long would I stay with that northeast trail? Not long. Where he would make his decision, as I was making mine, was at the base of a V, and the two sides spread out rapidly. If he stayed long with the right-hand trail he would lose time getting back to the other.

Or would he think it out the way I was thinking, and figure I'd really aim to make it on the left-hand trail?

I took a chance and started up the left-hand trail toward the mountains. And I found no tracks. I scouted right and left, but I still found none. I'd been fairly outguessed, outsmarted, and left miles behind. Nevertheless, I had to think of a night camp, and for some time I'd been seeing the tracks of antelope or wild burros or horses heading toward a blunt brow that thrust out from the main body of the mountains. There was no trail that I could see leading that way, but the chances of water were good, so I followed the next set of tracks.

The late afternoon was still. High overhead a buzzard circled, but he had no interest in me today.

The shadows were long when I found where the tracks converged at Barrel Spring in a corner of the mountain where there was quiet. I heard a few doves . . . nothing else.

The water was cold and good. I filled my canteen first . . . a man never knew when he might have to run, and I wanted a full canteen. Then I drank, and allowed the grulla to drink. He put his nose deep into the water, pulled it out, shook his head with pleasure, and then he drank.

A dim trail came down along the small stream back of the spring. Not liking the look of it, I walked up a short distance, until I found a cove shielded by some brush. I went back and got my horse and picketed it on the grass there, hidden from sight of anything but the buzzard.

Chewing on some jerky, I returned to the spring for another drink, brushed out my tracks in the sand, trying to leave no sign that anyone had been there. Then I went back behind the brush with my horse and bedded down in the soft sand.

Lying there with my pistol at hand, I considered the situation. About a day's ride to the north—perhaps a day and a half—was the stage route to Salt Lake and points east. There was a town up there, and further along the stage route was Eureka, a booming town of mines, mills, theatres, and saloons.

If Pony had gone up the valley he would be heading for Eureka, or cutting back to Austin . . . which I thought was the name of the town to the north. If the latter, I had a good chance to cut him off there and get my horse back, and my guns. To say nothing of the money in my saddle-bags.

If he rode east . . . well, I was going that way, anyway.

And so, if I had guessed right, was Bob Heseltine.

CHAPTER 20

Something prodded me in the stomach, and instantly I was awake. I was angry and started to speak, but the shape of that hat against the night warned me.

It was Pony, and he had me again.

"You just set tight, stranger, until I have a look at you—"

I heard a match strike, and my hand beside my blankets closed on a handful of sand. He was leaning forward, his rifle held in his right hand. He would kill me the moment he recognized me. He was just making sure, and . . .

My hand shot up and let go with the sand in his eyes. He gave a low screech and the match went out, and I swept the rifle muzzle up with the other hand. The gun went off and I was on him, punching and striking hard.

Somehow he lost his grip on his rifle, but we came up fighting. I hit him in the mouth and he staggered, reaching for his hip. I went in fast, punching with both hands, and he never got the gun out. He went down, tried to roll aside, and I kicked, catching him in the belly.

He grunted with pain, but there was no quit in the man. We both were fighting for our lives, and he came up clawing at my eyes. I leaped back, almost tripped over a stone, and suddenly he grabbed up his rifle and was gone into the shadows.

Cursing myself for a fool, I pulled back into the brush, careful to make no sound.

His horses! They had to be close by, and on them were my money, my rifle, my guns.

Swiftly, I turned into the brush, caught up the picket rope of the grulla, and swung to its back. Gun in hand, I rode into the trail, saw the shadow of the horses below, and went down the trail at a run.

The horses stood at the spring, still saddled. I swung into my own saddle on the line-back dun, and leading the other horses, rode up the trail to the north. Behind me I heard a shout, then a shot that missed by yards, and then I was riding away at a good clip.

I now had my own horse back, and I had his horse, saddle, and outfit. Now his turn had come to walk. He had one advantage. He had his rifle . . . and he was not far from ranches and a town.

All night long I pressed on, switching from horse to horse. I cut across by a dim game trail to Indian Valley, ate a good breakfast from some of Pony's carefully bought supplies, and then I rode out along the bank of the Reese River, heading north.

He wouldn't quit, I was sure. I had bested him and he would come after me, and for as murderous a man as he was, he would have no trouble getting a horse. He would simply shoot the first man he saw with one.

My money was still in the saddlebags, and with it a small poke of gold.

Men took a long look at me when I rode into Austin, but I paid no attention. I wanted to take a little time to get a good meal, and went into a restaurant.

The marshal came in, glanced at me sharply, and jerked his head toward the horses outside. "Two saddled horses, mister? You expectin' a friend?"

"I'm expecting a man, but he's no friend. Sit down, Marshal, and have some coffee." When he was seated I asked him if he had ever heard of Pony Zale.

"I've heard of him," he replied shortly. "What about him?"

"I left him afoot last night after he tried to kill me down near Barrel Spring. He'd robbed me and I was hunting him, but he found me asleep in the dark, and didn't know who I was. We had a tussle, and I lit out. As far as I'm concerned, I'm riding to Colorado as soon as I've finished eating."

"I'll keep an eye out for him, and you'd better, too.

If he comes up Big Smoky he might get ahead of you . . . that is, if he can lay hands on a horse."

When I left town at a good clip I headed east. Fifteen miles out I stopped for a breather, put my saddle on the grulla, and started again. All three horses were good stock, mountain-bred and used to long stretches of travel. I wasted no time. I didn't want to see Pony again, or so much as hear of him.

When I rode into Eureka it was a town ten or twelve years old, and there were eight or nine thousand people there, making a living from mining the lead and silver deposits.

As a town it was wild and woolly and hard to curry above the knees, with a hundred and twenty-five saloons and at least twenty gambling houses, all going full blast. In the past ten years they'd taken about $30,000,000 in silver out of the ground, and a quarter of a million tons of lead. Everybody was making money, and most of them were spending it as fast as they made it.

Stabling the three horses, I got them a bait of oats as well as hay, and then leaving my gear with the hostler I went down the street to a restaurant.

At the long table where I helped myself to mashed potatoes, slabs of beef, and several spoons of beans, I ate and listened to the talk.

"Never seen a man so quick," a man was saying. "I've known Pete for years, and figured he was as good with a gun as a man can be, but he never had a chance."

"Gun battle?" I asked.

The man turned his head and looked at me. I was a stranger, but he was a talker with a story to tell. "Last night, outside the Bon Ton.

"A stranger, a well-set-up man, rode into town with a blonde woman. Pete, he was feeling his oats a mite and he braced this stranger. The man tried to walk away from him, but Pete yelled after him and reached for his gun. Pete's killed a couple of men, and he was feelin' mean. Well, he never got off a shot. This stranger put two bullets into his heart and then just walked off down the street."

"Bob Heseltine," I said.

"Heseltine? No wonder Pete never had a chance. You say that was Bob Heseltine? The man Shell Tucker is chasing?"

"It sounds like him," I said, and filled my cup again.

Heseltine had been here last night, might even still be here. But what about Kid Reese?

"You mentioned a woman? Wasn't there another man with him, too?"

"Come to think of it, one of the boys was sayin' there was a man rode in with him. He's taken sick, or something. I hear he's over to Doc Macnamara's place."

When I'd finished eating I went outside. It was sunny and bright, quite a few people were walking up and down, and there were several rigs and saddle horses around. I stood under the awning in front of the theatre and studied the town from under my hat brim.

Once I'd gotten my outfit back I'd shifted into some better clothes, but the trip had been hard on the duds and it was time I picked up some jeans and a coat. The weather was turning cold in the evening.

Down the street I saw Doctor Macnamara's sign. After a moment I strolled down to his office door, and stepped inside. His waiting room smelled of stale cigar smoke, and there was a worn copy of the *Police Gazette* on a stand, along with a *Harper's* and several week-old newspapers.

The door to the inner office was partly open, and the doctor thrust his head out. "Be with you in a minute. If you're bleeding, stand off the carpet. I just paid fifty cents to have it cleaned."

"I wanted to ask about a patient of yours."

"Which one? Most of the folks around here have been patients of mine. Trouble is this here country's too healthy for me to make a living. Why, over at Pioche they had to shoot a man to start a graveyard."

"The man I am asking about is Kid Reese. Came in here a day or two ago, with another man and a blonde woman."

"Him?" He studied me for a moment, his eyes suddenly alert. "Are you a friend of his?"

"No," I said bluntly, "we've shot at each other a couple of times. I want to know what kind of shape he's in, and I want to talk to him."

"Have you been traveling with him?"

"Chasing him," I replied.

"I won't have any trouble around here. Anyway, he's

a sick man . . . a very sick man."

"What's wrong with him?"

"Stomach trouble, he says. My guess is arsenic poisoning."

"Arsenic? From bad water?"

"I doubt it. A man would have to drink more often than he has from one spring to get all he's had. I think somebody has been feeding it to him for quite a while."

Ruby Shaw . . . ! Well, that would be one way of getting rid of him.

"He said he only had one enemy he knew of, and that enemy hadn't been anywhere near him in some time. I told him in a case like this you didn't worry about your enemies, but those you thought were your friends."

"Can I see him?"

The bedroom off the office had four beds for patients. Only one of them was occupied, and the man who lay in it was Kid Reese, all right, or what was left of him.

His face was thin, his features were drawn, his eyes hollow. He stared at me, and then reached under his pillow as if for a gun.

"I'm not going to shoot you, Kid," I said. "Looks to me as if you've got trouble enough."

"I got nothing to say to you."

"At least I didn't fill you full of arsenic."

"That's a lot of nonsense. Who could do that? Who would have any reason to?"

"What about Ruby, Kid? Without you, she'd have Heseltine and the money, and with Bob—"

"Are you crazy? Ruby? How could she? And anyway, she dotes on Bob. You're tryin' to fill me with bad thoughts about my friends. You just wait until—"

"How could she? I'll lay you five to one she's been making the coffee lately. And the kind of coffee we drink out here is poisonous enough without adding arsenic. And I'll bet she hasn't been drinking much of it herself."

"That's a damned lie! That's—" His voice trailed off, and his brows drew together with sudden awareness.

"I don't want you, Kid. I want my money, and I'm going to get it."

Deliberately, I sat down. Doc Macnamara looked at Reese, and then he said, "I know nothing about your troubles. There is arsenic in some of the water out here, but not enough to poison you the way you have it. I would say—and I have had such cases before this—that you had been fed increasing doses over quite a period of time."

The doctor shrugged. "However, I am surmising. I would have to perform an autopsy—"

"Not on me, you don't!" Suddenly Reese said, "Doc, am I going to get well?"

"I think so. That is, if you don't get any more of it. This man is supposed to be your enemy, I believe, but if I were you I'd take his advice and never go near those people again."

228

He didn't like it, but it was obvious that he believed us. He had believed me even before the doctor spoke, because evidently he remembered who had been making the coffee.

"I ain't got any of your money," he said, his tone surly. "They're takin' care of it for me."

"I'll bet," I said dryly.

"You think I'm a damn fool, don't you?" he said.

"Nobody has a corner on being a fool, Kid. We were all fools back there in Texas when we stood around shooting off our mouths about how big and tough we were going to be. You two were fools when you tied in with Heseltine, and he was seven kinds of a fool for going to Ruby Shaw with that money. I'll bet she's argued against you dividing it, all along."

"Maybe she has. That cuts no ice."

"What will you do when you get out of here, Kid? Go back to them? Will you have the guts to warn Heseltine that he'll be next?"

Reese was silent. The doctor went into his office and began puttering over some papers.

"Where are they, Kid? I owe those folks back in Texas and I want to get my money."

Reese did not answer for a minute, then he said, "You'd go against Heseltine? You actually would?"

"Of course." Even as I said it, I suddenly realized that I would do just that. A lot had happened to that boy who had left Texas on a cattle drive. And then I added, with sudden surprise to realize it was true,

"Bob Heseltine will be more worried about facing me than I will about facing him."

He looked hard at me. "You figure you've put on some weight, don't you?" But he didn't sneer. I could see that Kid Reese believed it, too. "I won't deny," he added, "that Bob's almost had his fill of you—you hangin' on his trail and all. He ain't sleepin' so well any more. Fact is, none of us have been."

He turned his eyes on me. "If I cut free of them, will you lay off me?"

"I don't want you, Kid. I never did. You knew that was our money and you knew that was our horse, but I just want the money back."

"What did those folks in Texas ever do for you?"

"Nothing." But then I said, "I take that back. They did do something for me—or for pa, which is the same thing. They trusted him. You'll find out that counts for a lot, Kid, a lot more than buying drinks for a lot of rum-pots or shady women to show how big a man you are."

"Maybe you're right. All right, I'll tell you something. Bob Heseltine's got him a hideout up back of Bridal Veil Falls, near Telluride."

"Where's Telluride?"

"It's a new camp. A man named John Fallon staked some claims up there, and she looks like she's going to boom."

That was all I got out of him, and I was not too sure of that. He had no reason to tell me the truth, and enough reason to lie. On the other hand, somebody

230

had been feeding him arsenic, and perhaps he already knew what had happened to Doc Sites.

Two days I stayed on in Eureka, scouting the town, making inquiries. Heseltine and Ruby had been in town, all right, but they had pulled out, headed east.

I switched horses and went after them, making good time. Several times I thought I was coming up to them, but each time it turned out to be some other people.

It was a wild and beautiful land through which I rode, but the trail was becoming crowded. Three times during the first day I passed freight outfits, and several riders passed me, as well as a stage going each way. It was getting so a man could scarcely ride five miles on that trail without seeing somebody.

In Utah I sold Zale's horse, but I had become too attached to the dun and the grulla to let them go.

That day had been a cool one, and I was wearing a short thick wool coat when I rode up to the stage station. It was getting on for evening and I was hunting a place to stay. The station stood in the open without so much as a cottonwood tree nearby. Just a stone corral, the stone house and the trail that bent in toward its door.

There was a water trough and I rode up to it. A man peered from the doorway then came over.

"Howdy! Passin' through?"

"Maybe. Have you got some good food in there?"

"Sort of. Fact is, I've got me a new cook, if she'll stay. That's what I came out for. She's lookin' to buy

231

a hoss, and I was wishful you'd not sell her one of yours. I see you've got an extra."

"I'm keeping my horses."

I tied them, and as an afterthought, considering what he'd said, I tied them double tight. When somebody wants a horse real bad there's no use putting temptation in their way.

He went ahead of me, and when he stepped through the door he said, "Ruby, there'll be another mouth for supper."

It was Ruby Shaw.

She saw me at the same minute I saw her, and her face went cold and hard. She began to swear, and she could swear better than any mule-skinner I ever did hear. I stood quiet a minute, and then I said, "Mister, I'll not stay for supper, and if I was you I'd not eat her cooking either. The last man she cooked for is dying of arsenic poisoning."

"Damn you!" She spat the words at me. "Damn you to hell! You turned a good man into a yellow dog!"

"Not me," I said. "You."

I turned around and went back to my horses, and the man followed me. "What was all that about? Do you know her?"

"Her name is Ruby Shaw. She must have come in here with a man. What happened to him?"

"He left, right after she fell asleep. He was not a well man, if you ask me. He stopped out there, right where you stand, all knotted up with pain and holdin' his belly. When I asked him about the woman, he said I

232

was to keep her or get rid of her, and then he lit out. He took her horse, too."

Untying my horses, I thought bitterly of a cold camp somewhere in the mountains or desert ahead, then I swung my leg over the saddle and was off.

She came to the door and called after me, but I did not look back.

CHAPTER 21

If Bob Heseltine figured on hiding out in the mountains near Telluride he had better hurry. The season was getting on and that was country where the drifts piled deep. Once back in those mountains, he would be there for the winter, unless he was a good man on skis or snowshoes, and had them with him.

Skis were something I'd never attempted, but men who carried the mail through the mountains had been using them for years; and out California way, Snowshoe Thompson had made himself a reputation carrying the mail on them.

There'd been a growing chill in the air that made me think of hunting a hole. If I was going to see Vashti before snow flew I was going to have to forget about Heseltine and make time.

Frost had turned the leaves, and the mountainsides were splashed with golden clouds of aspen. Great banks of them poured down the steep slopes as though the earth had suddenly decided to give up and pour all her gold out to the waiting hands of men, only this gold was there for everyone to have—they had only to look. It was the kind of wealth that stayed with a man down the years, the kind you could never spend, but the memory of it waited in your mind to be refreshed when another autumn came.

I was going home, I was thinking now. Home? Well, for me home was where Vashti was, and it had taken me a while to know it. The only trouble was, would she still be there? Would she think of me as I did of her?

All the time I'd been covering country I'd seen a lot of men who had settled down to building businesses for themselves. Here I was, wasting time chasing after a couple of thieves when I should have been building something for myself.

Men were ranching, farming, mining. They were making names for themselves like those Yankees who came first to California, men who were going to be respected when most of the gun-packing lot were only remembered . . . remembered, but ignored.

Well, it was all right to sing in the sunshine, but I'd seen too many old men sitting on porches in their shabby clothes to want to be one of them.

Respect those men who were doing things to make a future? You bet I did. Most of them were busy building, opening new country, and making it better for those who would come after. They'd done the hard work, built the roads, opened the mines, dug the wells, guarded the cattle, and built the railroads. I was willing to do my share, but I wanted to be there when the payoff came.

The trail made a turn and there ahead of me was a crossroads settlement, half a dozen buildings, and a stage coming my way that had just stopped. The dust hadn't even settled, nor the dogs stopped barking.

Folks were starting to get down from the stage when the dun ambled up to the hitchrail and I stepped down from the saddle.

It wasn't much of a place. The stage stop was also a saloon and a restaurant. There was a corral, a couple of shacks and a second saloon. There was also a place with a sign over the door that said BEDS in big letters.

A square-built man with a square, hard-jawed face was standing on the porch watching the passengers step down. He turned to me as I walked up, brushing the dust from my coat. He was wearing a badge.

"Shell Tucker?"

"Yes."

"Come inside."

He went behind the counter, opened the door of a big old iron safe and took out a sack. He put it on the counter in front of me.

"A man came in here, sold his horse, and bought a ticket on the stage. Then he came over to me, bought me a drink, and put this sack on the table.

"He said, 'In a few hours, or maybe in a couple of days, there'll be a man named Shell Tucker come riding in here.' He described you mighty well. 'When he comes in you tell him to take this and lay off. . . . Just tell him to lay off.'

"I asked him if he was Bob Heseltine, and he said he was, and then he said, 'I can't keep runnin' all my life. A man's got to be able to sleep, he's got to be able to rest. I've tried outrunnin' him, and it didn't work out. We tried killin' him, and he won't be killed. I got to have some sleep, sometime. You just give him this and tell him to lay off.' "

"Thanks," I said. "I wish he'd done this months ago . . . a long time ago."

"Well, he's done it now. You going to lay off?"

"Why not? I never wanted him. I have to pay this money—or most of it—to some folks down in Texas."

The man with the badge nodded. "Can I buy you a drink?"

"Looks as if I'm the one should do the buying."

The bartender brought a bottle to the table. "I want coffee, too," I said, "and whatever is left to eat."

"There's a-plenty," he said. "The stage wasn't carryin' many folks. Just an old man and a girl."

The door opened for the last of the passengers, and I looked up. And there in the door was Vashti. Vashti and her pa.

"Shell! Oh, Shell!" she said, and she came right into my arms, and it seemed the natural thing to do.

Lander Owen seemed older, more tired. But he looked at me, grinning. "Looks as if you stepped into a loop, boy."

"What are you doing here?"

"I was hurt in a rockfall, and the doctor told me I should go to a warmer climate. I told him I thought I was heading there, and he said I shouldn't wait until I died, but to go now. So we're on our way."

"Con told us you were in Los Angeles," Vashti said.

"I'll turn right around and go back," I said.

The man with the badge had gone out, and only the stage driver was left. He had walked to the bar for a drink and was talking to the bartender.

"I was coming to look you up," I said to Vashti and her pa. "I've got my money back and I'm through with all that."

"You're damned right you are!"

Bob Heseltine was standing just inside the doorway, and he was all squared away to kill me.

"Get out of the way, Vash," I said quietly.

"I thought you'd gone, Bob," I said. "I thought you'd quit."

"Like hell! I figured to, and then I got mad all over again and said I'll be damned if I do!"

"You've still got a chance, Bob," I said. "The road is out there and you can ride. I don't want anything from you."

"You've played hell with me," he said. "*Me!* Bob Heseltine! I should have killed you the first time I saw you!"

"Your horse is out there, Bob. There's no need for this now."

He was staring at me. "Why, damn you! I could pull a gun faster than you when I was six!"

"Reese is going to make it, I think, Bob," I said, still speaking quietly. "He had a good doctor and he was drinking lots of milk and taking it easy. And I saw Ruby back where you left her. She was cooking for the stage tender."

"Cooking? *Her?*"

"That's right. I—"

He went for his gun and I beat him.

My gun slid into my hand with an easy motion. I had no sense of hurry, no fear. This was the moment for which I had been preparing myself for a long time.

His hand went down, his gun came up, and I shot him in the belly, shooting three times, as fast as I could slip the hammer, a steady roar of sound, with no breaks.

Heseltine got off only one shot—into the floor.

He went to his knees, started to get up, then just rolled over. It was a moment, a long moment, before I could believe he was dead.

Suddenly the man with the badge was in the doorway. "He came back," I said. "He came back."

"I thought he would," he said.

The stage driver stuck his head in the door. "Stage leaving," he said. "All who're going, get aboard."

"Get on," I told Vashti and her pa. "You get aboard. I'll ride along after."

And that was how I returned to California.

FOOTNOTES

1. David May founded the May Co. stores.
2. Meyer Guggenheim founded the Guggenheim fortune here.
3. Thomas Walsh was the father of Evelyn Walsh McLean, owner of the Hope Diamond.
4. The area now called Hollywood; known then as La Nopalera.
5. Now known as Wilshire Blvd.

Center Point Publishing
600 Brooks Road ● PO Box 1
Thorndike ME 04986-0001 USA

(207) 568-3717

**US & Canada:
1 800 929-9108**